BUZZARDS AND BLOOD

Shiloh took in a deep breath, let half of it out, and prepared to fire. But before the Winchester's hammer fell, another shot rang out from the hills. The fat buzzard exploded in a shower of feathers.

"Hey, pardner! Nice shooting, eh?" came the cry from the rocks. "Yer next! Yer cain bet on it!"

The yell startled Shiloh more than the slain bird. It drifted over the windless desert, reaching Shiloh as little more than a whisper. It was the first time he had heard the voice of either gunman.

"Who are you?" he shouted back.

"Why ya wanta know who we are? Yer a dead man!"

Another shot exploded from the gunman, slamming harmlessly into the dead horse.

"You hear, dead man? Yer dead as that horse!"

The SHILOH Series
by Dalton Walker

SHILOH
SHILOH 2: DESERT HELL

SHILOH 3: BLOOD RIVAL
(coming in April)

DIAMOND BOOKS, NEW YORK

DESERT HELL

A Diamond Book / published by arrangement with
the author

PRINTING HISTORY
Diamond edition / January 1991

ISBN: 1-55773-452-6

Diamond Books are published by The Berkley Publishing
Group, 200 Madison Avenue, New York, New York 10016.

PRINTED IN THE UNITED STATES OF AMERICA

10 9 8 7 6 5 4 3 2 1

Dedicated to the Memory of
Barry Sadler
A Friend Who Left Us Too Soon

And to

Docs Carlon, Moreau, Maitlin, Rosenberg, Auld, and the sawbones and staff of *N5*. I owe you a debt that can never be repaid.

1

For a week—Sunday to Sunday—he had not been haunted by the dreams. The hard gray light of the slow-passing days blasted the memories from his head. And the cool nights brought only a dark and dreamless sleep. The dead had not followed him to this place.

Shiloh did not dare think that he was entering a time of grace. For to find even a small portion of salvation under the blazing sun in this lifeless, barren country was to admit a terrible secret truth.

The damned will find their own hell. They will search it out, no matter the cost.

Pulling lightly on the reins, Shiloh turned his horse down a narrow rocky trail from the top of the rise and toward the desert. Snorting in the dry air, the sweet-mouthed roan picked her way down the slope. She stepped carefully, gravel crunching beneath her feet as she emerged through the narrow cut at the rock-strewn edge of the desert.

Spread out before Shiloh lay a wasteland. Flat as a tabletop, it stretched toward the vague gun-metal blue shadows of distant mountains. He knew that to venture out too far into the open was madness. The hills at his back, now a day's ride away, held water and game. But the solitude beckoned Shiloh beyond reason. It called out to him in the absolute silence, save that of his horse's hooves on the gravel.

It was noon, and the sun had long stolen all but the most meager patches of shade. Above him a hawk rode lazy circles, then tilted its wing and angled off gracefully toward the hills.

Shiloh lifted one of the three canteens that hung from around the saddle horn. He had filled them by a stream that morning, before riding out east, into the angry red eye of the dawn sun. Uncorking the wooden container, he allowed himself a generous mouthful of the warm water. But even before he had the wood peg back in place, his lips were dry.

It was then that Shiloh saw them. There were three of them, circling high and slow in the cloudless sky. No more than smudges against the blinding blue; he had to squint against the noon sun to count them.

"Well, goddamn," Shiloh whispered to himself. Had they not been so far off he would have felt that the buzzards were circling for him.

And then Shiloh saw the rider. He was a good mile off to the south, a distant image that shimmered in the heat. Shiloh pulled up on the reins and studied the scene.

Now, he knew, it was death leading him into the desert. He could feel its presence, as familiar as the saddle he sat on or the clothes he wore.

Riding steadily, Shiloh angled off into the flat, sun-blasted land. He could feel the sweat rolling down his back. Even as he approached the rider, the buzzards drifted slowly down. Shiloh kneed his horse gently, wanting to make it to the man before the birds.

When he was close enough, Shiloh called to the shimmering image of the rider, but his voice vanished in the great empty expanse that lay before him, sucked up by the deadening silence of the desert.

As the buzzards circled lower, Shiloh could see that the man was slumped over in the saddle. His horse walked at its own whim, bowing down lazily every few yards to sniff among the dried brush. The rider was not wearing a hat, and a large bandanna drooped low across his chest.

The sun must have gotten to him, Shiloh thought. Again he examined the buzzards, who circled with infinite patience against the sky.

When he was nearly close enough to see the man's face, Shiloh nudged his horse forward, closing the distance between him and the rider at a slow trot. Calling again, he could see the slumped figure turn his head slowly toward the noise before dropping it heavily back toward his saddle.

Shiloh called twice more, raising his hand in greeting as he approached the rider. Then, when he was nearly on him, the lone rider again turned his head toward the sound of Shiloh's voice. Shiloh pulled up his reins at the sight.

The rider was not wearing a bandanna. It was blood that covered the front of his shirt. The stain extended down from his jaw to his belly. Shiloh had seen such stains before, on dead men. It was the kind of mess that was made by a man with a cut throat. The ugly wound gaped like a second mouth across his neck, caked with blood and dust.

Riding closer, Shiloh could now see that the man had taken a half-dozen turns with the reins around his wrists, securing them to the bloody pommel. His nose had been smashed flat against his face, the flesh spread out nearly to his cheeks. A smooth, bloodstained finger of cartilage poked through the crushed nose. The sun had burnt the skin off his bruised and swollen face. Large blisters swelled across his neck and cheeks. His lips were nearly black.

He was no more than a boy, not even twenty.

Pulling alongside the rider, Shiloh grabbed the reins. The horse stopped at once, the action causing the dying man to again turn his face toward Shiloh. His eyes, though nearly swollen shut, blazed bright red. They were the same eyes that Shiloh had once seen on a cowman in Kansas who had rubbed Bull Durham into the corners as a rouser, to keep from falling asleep on the trail. They were the eyes that Shiloh had imagined the devil himself might have.

"You have water, stranger?" the rider asked in a dry whisper. "I sure would be obliged."

When the rider could not untangle his hands from the reins, Shiloh reined his horse closer and held the canteen up to the swollen, blackened lips.

The boy drank greedily from the canteen, water escaping from either side of his mouth and running down his chest to mix with the dried blood.

Shiloh pulled the canteen away slowly when the boy began to gag.

"I'm obliged," said the stranger, studying Shiloh with those horrible red eyes. "You just got yourself a friend for life."

"We gotta find you some shade," Shiloh said, sealing the canteen and stepping down from his horse.

"I would surely be obliged," came the young man's response. But it was the voice of a man past caring. Had it not been for the dry, rasping whisper, he could have just as easily been thanking Shiloh for giving him the time of day.

"What's your name, son, and how in hell did you get

out here?'' Shiloh asked, running a length of rope through the dying man's bridle.

''Phillip Malley,'' came the reply.

The first shot hit Malley's horse in the hind quarters, bringing its back end down fast and its front end up in an eye-rolling cry of pain. Shiloh heard the blast and horse's cry at the same time.

The second shot took off most of Malley's knee, knocking the dusty boot from the stirrup and nearly severing the leg before burying itself in the animal's chest. A bright foam of blood erupted from the animal's mouth as its front end collapsed under buckling legs.

For a brief moment Malley turned a questioning gaze to Shiloh. Then those red Bull Durham eyes changed from wonderment to fear as they struggled against the swollen flesh to open wider. ''Oh, dear God, them sonsabitches found me,'' Malley whispered in the same dry voice.

Shiloh pulled the Winchester from his saddle boot. The gunfire was coming from the rocky hills, but Shiloh could see nothing, not even a trace of powder smoke. ''Who is that? Who is that shooting at us?'' Shiloh asked, lowering the rifle as he began struggling at the leather that held the young man's hands to the pommel.

Then there were two more shots. The first hit Malley square in the side, lifting him slightly up off the worn leather of the saddle before his bound hands pulled him back down. The second took off his jaw in a spray of blood and bone that shone bright for an instant against the gray hills.

Shiloh rolled over the haunches of the fallen horse. Then another shot sang out from the rocky hills and the animal snorted in pain and rolled over, as dead as its rider. For a moment Shiloh was face-to-face with the dead man. The bright red eyes stared out of the mangled face. Now they looked neither surprised nor fearful. They hardly looked human, more like the eyes of a slaughtered steer.

Shiloh tore his gaze away from the grotesque sight and lifted his head cautiously over the top of the dead animal. Pumping a cartridge into his rifle, Shiloh surveyed the scene. It was three hundred yards to the rocks.

As the desert's silence closed in around Shiloh, he studied the hills for signs of the gunmen. There were at least two of them, of that much he could be certain. The last two shots were too close together to be the work of one man.

Then another shot sounded from the hills. This time Shiloh saw the gray smoke rise from behind a large boulder as his horse cried out in pain. The bullet had struck the roan square in the neck, sending her to the ground in a paroxysm of pain. Her hooves beat frantically in the dirt, stirring up a small gray cloud of dust as a dark fountain of blood rose from the wound.

In a cursing fury, Shiloh pumped off five rounds toward the rocks. But it was in vain. Even if he could have seen the gunmen, the Winchester was all but useless at this distance.

Two more shots rang out from the hills, thumping heavily into Malley's dead horse. Shiloh could see now that the gunmen were close together.

Shiloh squeezed off three more rounds toward the rocks, then reloaded from the .44 shells on his belt. Crawling on his belly, he began working his way to his saddlebag for more cartridges. The dying horse's breath came in a moist rattle, her flank shivering in spasms, as her eyes gaped open with numbing pain and fear.

As he rose slightly between the two horses, another shot exploded from the rocks, saving Shiloh the mercy bullet to put his animal away. The bullet had ripped through the worn leather fender of the center-fire rig and into the animal's heart.

Shiloh could feel the animal's last shuddering spasms beneath his arm as he unknotted the saddlebag strap and dug inside for more cartridges. His hands searching frantically in the darkness of the saddlebag, Shiloh felt the small sacks of Pinkerton gold, a whetstone, and a tobacco tin slide beneath his grasping fingers before finding the paper boxes of cartridges.

Tearing open the boxes, Shiloh scooped out three fistfuls of the brass cartridges. They spilled out across the leather and down his horse's hind quarters. It was then that he felt the dampness seeping through at his thighs and realized the worst of it. The horse had fallen on the canteens, crushing at least one of them and releasing its precious contents to the scorched earth of the desert.

Now there was nothing left to do but wait. It would be a near-moonless night, and at dark he might be able to circle toward the rocks. Looking skyward, Shiloh could once again see the slowly circling buzzards.

2

FOR A LONG time the desert lay in silence around Shiloh. The sweet promise of solitude that had whispered in his head, beckoning him to this place, had vanished. Fate had led him on, with a whore's promise. But still, he could see the terrible beauty of it as the lowering sun bled against the western horizon, turning the distant mountains black as pitch. No more shots sounded from the rocks as the diminishing light cast the rocky hills before him into shadow. When the air began to cool, Shiloh ventured an arm over the back end of his horse and retrieved his woolen coat, pulling hurriedly at the knots that secured it and the tightly wrapped bedroll.

The buzzards landed at sunset. Impatience and the sight of Malley and the dead horses had finally lured them downward. Their great black wings beating, they let their fat bulk fall awkwardly to earth several yards from where Shiloh waited.

Studying the birds in the growing darkness, Shiloh pulled his arms into the faded Union coat and waited.

So this is how it begins again, Shiloh thought, awed by

the cruel ingenuity of his fate. Even in this strange and desolate land, it's still the same. Now it wasn't fear that crept up on him, even as the buzzards waddled closer, their ridiculous small heads twitching this way and that. It wasn't fear, but anticipation that crashed and rang in his ears like a long train passing with its slow thunder of noise. He could feel his heart pounding in his chest and see the rocky hills before him with clarity. He already longed to be done with the killing he knew would come. Every muscle in his body tensed with the waiting. And even in the lengthening shadows, he could see the rocky hills before him with near-painful clarity.

The fattest of the birds waddled closer. Shiloh could hear its long gray claws scraping the ground with each shuffling step. Its cautious clucking rose from somewhere low in its long, thin throat. Shiloh ran his hand down the smooth stock of the Winchester. It would be easy work, shooting them now.

Raising the barrel of the rifle, Shiloh pressed his cheek against the cool wood and curled his finger around the trigger. Sensing that something was wrong, the fat bird retreated to consort with its comrades.

When the bird stopped waddling, Shiloh brought his sight drifting slowly down until it was lined up with the bird's great, black-feathered body.

Squeezing the trigger slowly, Shiloh took in a deep breath, let half of it out, and prepared to fire. But before the Winchester's hammer fell, another shot rang out from the hills. The fat buzzard exploded in a shower of feathers. The force of the bullet sent it pinwheeling for several yards past its frightened comrades, already beating their wings toward flight, to where it fell lifeless to the ground.

"Hey, pardner! Nice shooting, eh?" came the cry from the rocks. "Yer next! Yer cain bet on it!"

The yell startled Shiloh more than the slain bird. It drifted over the windless desert, reaching Shiloh as little more than a whisper. It was the first time he had heard the voice of either gunman.

Lowering the rifle, Shiloh cupped his hands to his mouth. "Who are you?" he shouted back, his voice sounding weak and thin in the empty expanse.

"Hey, pardner! Why ya wanta know who we are? Yer a dead man!"

Shiloh brought the rifle around and let the sight slide over the rocky hills before him. Another shot exploded from the gunman, slamming harmlessly into the dead horse.

"Yer a dead man! You hear? Yer dead as that horse!" This was another voice, younger and almost laughing.

Shiloh fired twice toward the voice in the rocks. Then the desert fell quiet. Soon it would be dark as a well. A small waxing moon hung low in the darkening sky over the hills.

When it was completely dark, Shiloh made his way back, away from the horses and into the desert. He duck-walked a hundred yards, then dropped to his belly and began to crawl. Moving slowly from brush to rock, he knew that he was an easy target.

Shiloh pulled his way across the ground like a snake, the Winchester in one hand. When he saw the two stones, no more than knee-high to a grown man, he rested, feeling the blood seep through the torn cloth at his knees and elbows.

Then Shiloh saw him. Turning toward the rocks, he watched as the figure rose slowly up near the dead horses. For the barest moment, he thought it was the boy, Malley, recovered from his wounds, as if in a dream. But then

Shiloh knew. It was one of the gunmen. He had come around the opposite side.

Shiloh jacked a shell into the rifle and rolled onto his belly. Bringing the shadow clearly into his sights, he fired.

The shot spun the man around, jerking the rifle from his hand. Firing again, Shiloh hit him square on, knocking him back off his feet.

Before the echo faded, Shiloh was on his feet and running toward cover—back to the slain horses. A half-dozen shots rang out from the hills, kicking up the dry dirt at Shiloh's scrambling boots and buzzing like angry bees around his head. When he was close enough, Shiloh dove headfirst behind the fallen horses.

"Yer a dead man," came the whisper. "Ya shot me good, but yer still a dead man."

The voice was so close that Shiloh could feel the moist breath against his cheek. Turning his head, he saw the face of the gunman. He was barely older than Malley. His lips were shut tight against the pain. Shiloh's first shot had hit him high in the shoulder. The second had caught him in the groin.

"Who are you?" Shiloh asked the dying boy as he slipped the youth's gun from its holster. "Why are you doing this?"

The young man opened his eyes wide to stare at Shiloh and then he smiled. It was a small, twisted smile that made its way around a face contorted with pain. "Ya doan even know, do ya? Ya weren't with 'im."

Shiloh studied the boy. He was thin and slightly balding. His clothes—the shiny black pants, white and collarless shirt, that had once been a Sunday-best suit—were now stained and nearly worn through. "No, I wasn't with him," Shiloh said.

"Ya were just like passing by. Weren't ya, ya unlucky bastard?"

"Horace! You get him, boy?" came the shout from the rocks.

Shiloh studied the landscape down the barrel of his Winchester. To see a figure rise from the rocks would be too much to hope for.

"Horace! Speak up, boy!" came the call.

Shiloh came up on one knee and raised the rifle over his head. If he saw the figure, he could pull the gun down and get a shot off quickly.

"Damn, that ain't gonna fool nobody," the dying boy taunted in a groan. "Yer still a dead man."

"Shut that mouth," Shiloh hissed as he waved the rifle.

"I reckon I'll be quiet soon enough, ya bastard," came the answer in a bitter whisper.

"Horace, you come up where I can get a look at you," the gunman in the rocks called.

"The boy's hurt," Shiloh shouted back. "You come down and get him."

There was a long silence from the rocks before the gunman answered, "Horace, can you hear me?"

Looking down, Shiloh saw that the boy was dead. He had died without a whimper or a prayer. His pale face stood out in sharp contrast against the darkened ground.

"Horace, can you hear me?" the voice called again.

"He can't talk," Shiloh replied. "He's dead."

Five quick shots sounded from the rocks. They thumped evenly into the dead horse. Shiloh could feel each one hit with a slight shudder that passed through the slain animal where he rested the Winchester. Instinctively, he tightened his finger around the rifle's trigger, then made himself ease off, knowing he would need the cartridges.

The gunman in the rocks remained quiet after that. Shiloh guessed that he would be waiting for a shadow or a movement, anything that would give away his location.

When an hour or more had passed, Shiloh began moving again. Working his way on his belly, he made his way back, a half mile or more, past the rocks where he had found cover before, then West for another quarter mile. It took him a long time to reach his destination, a small arroyo, barely deep enough to provide decent cover in daylight. But if the gunman had not changed his position, Shiloh would be well out of rifle range.

If it was sleep that visited Shiloh as he lay in the narrow cut, he did not recognize it as such. The dreams returned as he stared toward the mute rocks and unseen gunman. The space between Shiloh and the rocks filled with Union and Confederate troops. Tennessee grass spread across the parched earth. And hell came calling . . .

Shiloh watches the battle from where he crouches. Unseen and fearful. His eyes burning from the thick smoke, he stares unmoving as butternut and Yankee clash. It is as he remembered it—that was the way it always came to him in the familiar horror of his dreams—nightmare disguised as memory.

Thousands died in a matter of hours. Now they are running. Young men running across the April grass, until unseen minie balls or grapeshot rips through uniform and flesh to send them to the ground in a horrible jerking dance. He can hear only the nearest ones cry out in pain. Others die with their last words—prayers and curses—drowned in thunder.

In his dream, Shiloh can feel his finger wrapped around the trigger, but cannot pull. Gaping wide-eyed at the slaughter, he watches as a young rebel is spun in his tracks. He is so close that Shiloh can hear the bullets crack through the bone of his chest and the rush of breath from his mouth. When he falls, he is looking directly at Shiloh. His eyes show no fear; death has not surprised him.

Shiloh recognizes the young reb as the boy, Horace. But he is not dead. Rather, his mouth twists into a mocking grin, ''Mister, yer an unlucky bastard,'' he laughs before dying.

When Shiloh wakes, it's with a start, a scream straining for a voice in his throat. The desert is the desert and the battle more than a decade in the past. But he can still hear the numbing thunder of guns in his ears. His eyes still burn with the powder-smoke. And the fear still pounds in his head.

Slowly, Shiloh pulls his cramped finger from around the trigger and looks out over the darkened rocks. A waking surge of fear runs through him. He knows that he could be dead. Sleeping, he would have been easy work for the unseen gunman.

3

IT WAS THIRST that sent Shiloh crawling again across the parched ground. His mouth was already dry, even in the cool predawn darkness. By noon the sun would turn the desert back into a sun-blasted landscape of hell.

He was certain now that only one gunman remained hidden in the hills.

Shiloh crawled slowly toward the rocks, the Winchester slung over his shoulder, the dead man's Springfield held in an outstretched hand. He moved slowly but at a steady pace, resting only when he came to the cover of a scrub. Once he reached the rocks he would have to move fast. It would be light then.

When he was nearly to the rocks, Shiloh looked back. In the gray dawn he could see the fallen horses outlined in the dim light; behind them, he knew, were the bodies of the two young men.

Shiloh covered the last few yards to the rocks quickly, his boots digging deep into the dry dirt. Then he allowed himself to rest between two stones that opened a small gap from the desert floor, ending in a small rincon of solid rock. His back propped against the cool stone, he listened for the sound of movement, a horse or boot step on gravel, but heard nothing.

The gunman, if he had not changed his position, was to his left, probably in a narrow cut, wide enough for horses.

Shiloh lifted his head and surveyed the steep hill. He saw nothing. Then, slowly, he began to climb the rock wall at its lowest point. His hand still wrapped around the Springfield, he wedged the toe of his boot into a crack and pulled his weight off the ground with one hand, using not more than his fingertips to grip a small crack above his head. When he had reached the top of the small cliff, Shiloh lay flat on his belly and viewed the rocky terrain down the barrel of the Springfield.

A hundred yards to his left he saw the horses. There were two of them, a chestnut and a gray paint, both saddled and ground-hitched in a narrow clearing. He could not see the gunman.

Working his way higher across the ridge, Shiloh caught his first view of the gunman. He was older than the boy, Horace. His shaggy hair was streaked with gray. He was asleep, wrapped in an Indian blanket. He slept sitting upright, leaning against a large stone. His rifle rested an arm's reach away, its barrel facing the desert, wedged between two stones so that a man wouldn't need to trust the steadiness of his own hands to shoot straight.

Bringing the Springfield up, Shiloh caught the sleeping gunman in his sights. It was not an easy shot, the man was boxed in on three sides in a small hidey-hole of stone away from the clearing and the horses.

Studying the outline of the sleeping gunman, Shiloh

knew that he had come up on the wrong side. The trail out was on the opposite side of the small clearing.

Shiloh kept the sleeping man in his sights. Then, slowly, the gunman woke. He stretched his arms, letting the blanket fall from around his shoulders. He wore a dirt-brown hat and worn brocade vest under a shabby broadcloth coat. Like the dead boy, he was wearing his go-to-town clothes.

Scratching his beard lazily, he rose. For an instant he was in Shiloh's sights. He swiveled his head, the two large eyes scanning the desert and turning. For an instant he seemed to look straight up the barrel of the dead boy's Springfield and straight into Shiloh's squinting eye. Then he unfastened the buttons of his trousers and stepped behind a large rock farther up the trail.

Keeping the rifle's sights trained on the spot where the gunman had sat, Shiloh waited. The horses nickered and stamped in the cool morning air, but the gunman did not return.

It seemed to Shiloh that he waited a long time, then he began making his way cautiously up the rocks. He moved slowly and silently, never taking his eyes from the gunman's camp as the sun rose at his back. But it wasn't until he was high up the hill, nearly to its crest, that Shiloh could see that the gunman was no longer there. He had simply walked away, leaving his rifle, the two horses, and an Indian blanket.

By the time Shiloh made his way down to the small clearing it was full light, and there was little doubt that the gunman had cleared out. He had just walked away as calmly and slowly as a man stepping behind a rock to relieve himself.

The camp contained nothing of value: the Indian blanket; another Springfield rifle, identical to the one Shiloh had taken off the dead boy; and the two horses, both with shabbily blotted brands. It was a camp that a man could walk easily away from.

The saddlebags held nothing but a half-dozen meat biscuits, a box of cartridges for the Springfield, and a few scraps of clothing. If there was a canteen, the gunman had somehow managed to take it with him.

Surveying the desert from the gunman's camp, Shiloh could see the buzzards had once again landed. Two fat ones had each claimed one of the horses, a third was busy out of view.

Untying the horses, Shiloh led them through the narrow cut in the rocks and down to the desert. It seemed a short ride to the horses and two dead boys. Shiloh shot the birds off their feast, squeezing off round after round from the Winchester without aiming. When the buzzard that had lighted on Malley's chest finally took flight, he trailed from his ugly beak a long red strip of flesh.

Malley had gotten the worst of it from the birds. They had begun on his face. Shiloh knew he would have to bury both Malley and the other one, Horace. The horses he would leave, rewarding the damned birds for their patience.

The paint and the chestnut were in poor shape. Lifting the chestnut's eyelid from its sunken eye, Shiloh saw that the white had turned a deep red from lack of water. So had its gums. The paint was worse. Pinching a portion of flesh at the animal's hind end, Shiloh saw that the small crease did not smooth back out.

Shiloh loaded the bodies of the two young men over the paint and tied them down with a length of rope. He knew that he should bury the boys proper, but it was a day's ride back to the hills and the small horse didn't look like he would make it. The animal had a split hoof as bad as any Shiloh had ever seen. Slightly sway-backed and ewe-necked, Shiloh guessed that the paint wasn't ever much good.

The horses both had the same blotted brand. Whoever had done the work wasn't much good either. Shiloh would have bet that the horses were stolen. When he opened Horace's saddlebag, he was sure of it.

Inside the boy's saddlebag, folded neat as a preacher's sermon, was a collection of wanted dodgers that marked the boy's trail from Utah, to California, to Nevada. Each poster offered a larger reward, all the way up to one hundred dollars. Horace had obviously been proud of his outlaw ways, even if the law that offered the rewards was markedly unenthusiastic about the young man's capture.

But it was the last poster that caught Shiloh's eye. It wasn't for Horace, but a pair of brothers out of Salt Lake. The reward was seven hundred dollars for the both of them.

Shiloh buried both men at the foot of the rocky hills, side by side. He wedged their bodies into a small crevice and covered them over with stones. When he was done, he knew that the birds or other wildlife couldn't get at them. It was thirsty work, and by the time Shiloh had finished, it was nearly noon.

Surveying the desert, he saw the birds feasting on the dead horses. There were a half dozen of them now, pecking and bickering under the sun for the choicest morsels. Then he began to ride, away from the desert and up into the hills.

By late afternoon Shiloh arrived at the first patch of shade. The gentle slope of green hills now lay before him. He was as thirsty as he had ever been. His mouth felt like cork, though he knew it would be nightfall before he could find water.

But what bothered Shiloh most was the gunman walking off like he did. It was as unexpected as a fifth ace in a poker deck. A man just doesn't wake up and light out with no thought to his gun or horse, unless he has good reason.

Looking back at the paint, he could see that the horse was having a hard time of it. The animal hobbled along, its neck pulled forward by the reins that Shiloh held in his free hand. Shiloh knew that he should just cut the lame horse free. Not only was it slowing him down, but riding one stolen horse was bad enough, without pulling another one behind him. Grimly Shiloh thought that if the law did find him and go against him, they could only hang him once.

As the trail turned upward, the paint began to stumble, its hooves catching on the rocks. It would be dark soon, but Shiloh would be damned if he'd lay his head down without getting a drink of water first. The green hills that lay before him darkened slowly, turning from lush green to black. At dusk they crossed a streambed, still damp with recent runoff from the hills. The horses looked forlornly down at the muddied strip, flaring their nostrils at the dim smell of water.

Shiloh studied the drying mud, already cracked in the hot, dry air. A day or two before it had been a stream that he could have rested at and drank from. It had carried the clear, sweet water of a summer storm that would have washed the dust from his face. In another week it might be a stream again.

And then he saw the tracks. The narrow streambed was just wide enough to cross in two strides and just moist enough to leave two near-perfect boot marks, drying in the desert air. Shiloh had no doubt who the tracks belonged to. Climbing down from the chestnut, he walked to the tracks. There wasn't a horse print in sight. They had to belong to the gunman.

"Well, goddamn," Shiloh whispered to himself as he knelt beside the footprints.

4

THE FOOTPRINTS LED out of the drying streambed toward a worn trace that ran straight and true up through the sparse trees into the hills. It would be easy work following the trail up into the greening hills.

Shiloh turned the chestnut with a hard pull of the reins and set off up the rocky trail. To his way of thinking, while the trail might not lead him to the gunman, it would surely lead him to water. It was then that he heard the first lonesome cries of coyotes. Their voices, far off, were carried by the cold, dry breeze down the slope. Where coyotes could live, so could a man. Following the trail in the failing light, he listened intently as the coyotes' mournful song grew nearer.

Shiloh saw the water at last light. A small pool had gathered in a rocky basin the size of a hat. Reining in the chestnut, he climbed down and led the animals to the pool. Shiloh spit the smooth pebble from his mouth and knelt beside the rock bowl that had collected the rainwater.

The hollow had caught perhaps two gallons of water from a recent rainfall. Now it waited for him as neatly as a bowl set out in a hotel room. Though its surface was clouded with dust, the water wouldn't have looked more welcome if it had been served up in a crystal pitcher by a Virginia City chorus gal. With the first taste of the tepid water, Shiloh felt the day's thirst fade from his mouth. When he had drank his fill, he splashed the water over his face and neck, then let the horses drink.

The water vanished quickly into the horses' lapping mouths. When there was perhaps a quart left, Shiloh pulled the paint and then the chestnut away from the precious find. The remainder he would save for breakfast the next morning.

It took a long time to gather enough wood for a fire. Shiloh knew that the foothills to the big Snow Mountains lay before him. Another day of riding would lead him to grassy fields where the horses could graze and he could hunt.

That night, sleeping on a hard bed of rock, the dreams returned. It had been a wet spring. The roads proved a torturous march, and the rivers ran muddied and swollen. But all was green. The trees were burdened with leaves and the grass was as sweet and thick as any that Shiloh had seen.

It was truly, he thought, a blessed land as they made camp by the log, one-room church meetinghouse. The Sibley tents grew quickly across the Tennessee landscape, the greening fields and lightly timbered woods became cities of gray canvas. Smoke rose from small fires and later from bakers' ovens as the smell of food mixed with that of spring in the clean, crisp air.

And the days had passed slowly. From the cool gray dawns to the lazy sunsets, more troops and supplies arrived from Pittsburg Landing. The sound of drums and bugles could be heard as officers drilled their recruits.

Some of the men fell sick from drinking the polluted river water and sweated the illness off wrapped in blankets. Home remedies only increased their misery as the surgeons scrambled good-naturedly from tent to tent to treat the ill-fated fellows with quinine.

But the boy, Henry Proffitt, stayed healthy. He was seventeen and eager to prove himself in battle—to die if necessary—fighting the Rebs. Then the fighting came.

In his dream Shiloh sees nothing. Smoke blankets the fields and fills the air between trees like a fog. In his dream the butternuts come through the gray gun smoke like grinning ghosts, rifles already up to their shoulders. Shiloh turns and runs, dropping his gun in the face of the advancing Rebs. Running blindly through the acrid fog, first in one direction, then another, like a frightened rabbit. But at each turn he faces another line of smiling Rebs. He runs until his lungs ache with each panting gasp of the thick smoke.

Even as he sees it in his dream, Shiloh knows it to be a lie. The Rebs did not smile, their faces showed only fear, a mirror of his own. And he did not run, instead he fought. He fought not for the Union, or Sherman, or Lincoln, but for his life, just as the Rebs were fighting for their lives.

The slaughter raged for hours. The gunfire rose to a deafening pitch, broken only by the cries of men and horses as they fell wounded to the trampled, blood-soaked ground.

The smoke cleared to reveal a nightmare. Thousands lay scattered across the open fields. Not even the trees escaped, their bare and broken branches stretched as ghastly markers against the graying sky at dusk. And the land that had once seemed blessed was turned to hell. From horizon to horizon stretched a vision fit only for the damned. Surely this had not been the work of fearful men, but of a vengeful, angry God.

The scene burned its way, like acid, into the young man's brain. It was then that Henry Proffitt was washed away, just as the night rain washed the blood from the corpses to lay naked their wounds and cleanse the powder smoke from their faces to reveal pale flesh set into masks of fear and pain. All that the young man had been and done and wanted was washed away. And it was from that place, an April field with its log church, that the man they would call Shiloh, wearing a tattered blue uniform, would walk. Numb and hollow-eyed, he did not know why he had not joined the dead. For certainly, since that day, he had grown to nearly envy them.

It was later that he would learn the fear. And it was later that he would fight the battle again. In fine hotels, under quilted covers, beneath star-crowded skies, sweating into his woolen bedroll and in the perfumed embrace of whores, the dreams would find him. And neither prayer, nor whiskey, nor a Chinaman's opium pipe would sweeten his sleep. Nor could money banish the memory of the dead.

Shiloh awoke in a sweat; the small fire by his feet had burned down to a pile of gray ash. It was dawn and the air had a bite to it. The horses stamped impatiently in the cold, waiting for a feeding that would not come.

Shiloh rebuilt the fire and allowed himself a length of salted jerked beef. Coffee would have tasted good, but there was not enough water. When he had finished the length of meat, Shiloh drank deeply from the remaining water, then led the chestnut to lap at the rest. The paint, he knew, would not be good for much longer. Only the fact that he was a day, or two at most, from plentiful water saved the crippled animal from a bullet.

It was a pleasant ride upward. By noon the sky cleared to a cloudless blue. The air was fresh and scented with pine and sage. But with each passing mile, the small paint stumbled more frequently. Its labored steps over the rocks finally drew blood that ran down the cracked hoof and left a thin crimson trail along the gently sloping path.

Shiloh had planned to trade the paint for food at the first ranch or let it free in a grassy pasture. With each painful step the creature took, Shiloh knew that a bullet would be the kindest thing. But the horse struggled along uncomplaining, pulling the lead rope taut as it hobbled along.

By afternoon the trail had steepened and narrowed. At times the path vanished, swallowed by trees that had somehow managed to sink roots into the rocky earth. Shiloh turned in his saddle to study the paint frequently. It walked in limping pain, the cracked hoof now a bloody mess, shattered by the climb over the unforgiving rocks.

Soon, Shiloh found himself promising the small horse death. "Get to that clearing, there," he urged the stumbling horse. "Just get to that clearing, then I'll use the gun. Just a little more." But as he reached each clearing, rise, and fallen tree, he found a new marker just ahead.

He could no more rest the Colt's barrel between those pained and pleading eyes than pull the trigger with that length of cool steel against his own flesh. To unsaddle the creature and lay it down with an echoing shot now seemed small reward for the pain.

And then he saw it. In a clearing ahead, three trails converged at a small stream. The water was no more than a trickle over the rocky bed, but that was enough. Shiloh turned in his saddle and studied the paint again. "You see that stream,'' he coaxed. ''Just make it to that damned stream.''

Urging the chestnut forward with a touch of his heel, Shiloh felt the lead rope grow tighter around the worn leather of the apple. Smelling the water, the chestnut pulled against the weight that held him, dragging the stumbling paint down, its good front hoof catching between two rocks. Shiloh heard the dry crack of bone as the ill-fated horse let out a long whimpering cry of pain.

The weight of the fallen horse stopped the chestnut in its tracks. Shiloh swung down from the saddle and walked back to where the paint lay across a clutter of rocks. It gasped, ribs heaving with the new pain of a broken leg. Running his hand lightly down the leg, Shiloh confirmed what he already knew. It was the cannon bone. Hardly ever a clean break, the thin bone had snapped and splintered, and now a bloodied white spear pointed out through the dappled flesh.

Now the chestnut was straining against the rope, nearly dragging the paint forward toward the stream. The rope, tight as a fiddler's string, pulled painfully at the paint's bridle. The small horse's eyes rolled backward with the pressure as the leather, remarkably, held.

Without thinking, Shiloh reached back and pulled his knife from the sheath. The sharpened blade cut through the stretched rope smoothly. As the final strands parted under the blade, the chestnut stumbled forward. Freed of the burden, he fairly pranced to the cool water of the mountain stream.

Shiloh watched as the thirsty horse bent its head to the water and drank. Too much water would bloat him useless, but what Shiloh had to do wouldn't take long. Bringing the gun from his holster, he clicked the hammer back with a smooth motion of his thumb. ''Just a few more steps and you coulda had some water,'' Shiloh whispered to the gasping animal. ''But that don't matter now, does it?''

Then Shiloh gently placed the barrel of the gun against the horse's speckled head and pulled the trigger. The paint quivered against the impact, its eyes bulging wide as its hooves beat and scraped against the rocky ground.

By the time Shiloh was on his feet, gun holstered, the horse was dead, though its haunches still twitched as if it were shooing flies. The shot brought the chestnut's head up from the stream. His large brown eyes turned to consider the scene behind him, and then he bent back toward the slow-running water.

Before drinking himself, Shiloh led the chestnut away from the water and tied him to a tree opposite the dead paint. Kneeling beside the stream, Shiloh drank. There was not enough water to scoop up a handful without skinning your knuckles, but it was enough.

5

WITH HIS HEAD bent to the slow-running water, Shiloh noticed the tracks. They were not the tracks left by a man on foot, but those of horses. Looking closely, he saw the scraped stone of horseshoes across the rock ledge bordering the stream. The markings were so recent, he could almost hear the sound of metal on stone.

With his hands still cupped with water, Shiloh rose to his feet. Now, he could see that the scrapings lined both banks of the narrow stream. Angling off in a crisscross of scarred stone, there were too many to be the work of one horse or even two.

Tracing a finger across the stone, Shiloh then saw that the scrapings led from a trail, obscured deliberately. It would not have been hard work on the rocky terrain to hide a trail. There were tricks—Shiloh knew many of them himself—from dragging branches to packing hooves with clay. But no trick could disguise those markings across the stone.

Studying the tracks more closely, Shiloh guessed that there were three riders, possibly four. They crossed the stream in a single line, one behind the other. Their horses probably crossed the narrow stream in two steps. Perhaps they paused here, as Shiloh had, to rest. If they had rode from the desert, this was the place they would fill their canteens.

But Shiloh had expected one man on foot. There was the chance that these tracks were made by a group of somebodies other than the gunmen from the rocks, but he doubted it. It was a straight line down the trail to the desert, a two-day ride with nothing between. And then it all made sense. A man would walk away from a horse and a rifle if he knew that another horse waited for him farther up the trail.

Shiloh studied the tracks like a map, but could not say for certain how many riders there were. More than two and less than six, of that he was dead sure.

Behind him, the chestnut whinnied and stamped impatiently, having exhausted the sparse supply of grass near its tether. It was about the sorriest-looking broom tail Shiloh ever sat on. Its skinny neck arched forward, and its goose-rumped hind end drooped lazily to the ground. And then there was an untrustworthy look about the horse. He would wait a month, a year, or three years, Shiloh suspected, for a chance at a clean kick at a man and would probably wait even longer to catch a finger or a hand between its blackened teeth.

It was the kind of animal a man rode 'cause he couldn't afford better, but it sure as hell wasn't the kind he stole. Even horse thieves, Shiloh knew, had their own fair share of pride in such matters.

As he prepared to leave, Shiloh studied the dead paint. He would leave the gunmen's saddle, saddlebags, and bedrolls, taking from them only the wanted posters, meat biscuits, and ammunition. The Springfields he would also pack, rigging an outfit low on the saddle that gave him the Winchester on one side and a pair of Springfields on the other. He would use his own saddle on the chestnut, as well as the saddlebags that held his gold.

When Shiloh had finally outfitted the beast, he unhitched the chestnut and climbed on wearily. It wasn't a surprise that he had to set the spurs to its side pretty good to get the animal moving. As they crossed the narrow stream, Shiloh tried to figure how far a lead the gunmen had on him. It was certainly more than an hour or two, perhaps as much as half a day.

"It should be you, you worthless sack of guts," he whispered gently to the chestnut. "Oh, yes, it should be you back there with an ounce of lead in your dim brain and flies buzzing 'round those lying eyes of yours."

The chestnut pricked up its ears at the sound of Shiloh's voice, and then, as if it understood the words, hesitated at a small crease in the rocky path. So perfect dead-on human was the animal's reaction that it caused Shiloh to tense, tightening his knees against the saddle's worn fenders.

There were those that said horses could understand a man's voice, even disguised in gentle tones, just like a woman could, but Shiloh never paid that much mind. Now, as the chestnut made its ill-tempered way up the mountain, Shiloh gave it a second and even third thought.

It might have been the extra weight of the rifles and gold the chestnut carried. Or it may have been the way that he reined the chestnut, with nice smooth movements that had little effect on the animal's tough mouth. But even as those thoughts passed through Shiloh's head, a part of him believed that the animal would turn on him given half the chance.

* * *

The tracks appeared again in late afternoon. It was as if the horses that made them were dropped down, out of the sky, to leave the prints in the trail's dirt.

Shiloh stepped down from the chestnut and led it a little ways up the path, stooping low to study the clear markings of the horses. He was only a fair hand at it, but he could see now that there were four horses. At the widest part of the trail they walked four across, their riders probably talking. Farther up the trail, Shiloh found a burned match.

It would be easy work now, following the riders. If they stayed on the lone trail and stopped to make camp, Shiloh could expect to meet up with them just after sundown.

Climbing back on, Shiloh put the spurs to the chestnut, setting him off at a fast walk. He didn't know who these jaspers were, but two of them had tried to kill him. They had put bullets into their rifles and shot at him. Now, one was dead and somewhere up the trail were the others.

As the climb became steeper, the chestnut complained more. At each turn the horse hesitated and balked at the pull of the reins. By sunset, Shiloh could no longer contain his hatred for the beast, cursing it loudly and digging his spurs back into its flesh. But even this did not improve its behavior. The damned thing was as stubborn as an army mule. It gave no quarter to the pain Shiloh inflicted on it by spur and rein. And it paid no heed to the curses he hurled. The chestnut tolerated it all with quiet contempt.

When it was nearly dark, Shiloh saw the smoke. It rose through the pines and carried west on a slight wind. Perhaps a mile up the twisting trail, Shiloh reined in the horse so savagely it brought its neck up in an angry, open-mouthed complaint. Common sense told Shiloh to hitch the horse to a tree and scout the camp, but he didn't.

Coming down off the chestnut, he led the animal slowly up the trail by its reins. Surprisingly, it moved willingly, once relieved of Shiloh's weight. When he was within a quarter mile of the camp, he saw the fire through the trees. It was a comfortable camp, set against a stone ledge on one side and a small stream on the other. The horses, four of them, were staked to the ground on the opposite side of the stream, their saddles off.

And then a man appeared. He walked from the shadows of the rock ledge and knelt by the fire, dropping into an easy crouch, his back end resting comfortably on his boot heels. He was wearing a faded brown coat and a black, low-crowned hat. Even at nearly a quarter mile, Shiloh knew he was not the gunman in the rocks. This one was a big man, lean and bony, he had the look of a nester or small-time rancher.

For a moment Shiloh thought that maybe he had made a mistake, maybe even followed the wrong trail and stumbled across the camp of four down-on-their-luck saddle tramps. And then he saw the gun stuffed into a cross-draw rig across the front of the man's trousers. It would have been the first thing you saw, meeting him on a street, and the first thing he wanted you to see.

Shiloh couldn't tell the make of the gun from where he sat in the bushes, but something about it, maybe the way the man carried it, pegged him as a hard case in Shiloh's mind.

Shiloh watched as the man fed the small fire to a blaze, carefully choosing the dry wood from a neat stack at his side. Then he placed a tin coffeepot near the center. Withdrawing a half-smoked cigar from his coat pocket, he brought a dry stick up from the edge of the cook fire and lit it. Rising again, cigar comfortably in his mouth, he walked back to the shelter of the rock.

Idly, Shiloh thought of the Springfield rifles. It would be easy work now. And somewhere, deep inside, he saw himself doing it. Go back to the horse. Get one of the rifles. Shoot the first one who comes out for a taste of coffee. Then shoot the others as they ran, stumbling and confused, from the darkness. He was downwind from the horses. It would be easy work getting himself close enough.

Shiloh rose slowly from his place in the bushes and walked back to the chestnut, keeping a hand on the Colt at his side. The Springfield faced him as he approached the horse. It was a tempting thought, killing the men just as they had tried to kill him. But there would be only small pleasure in it, just their surprised gazes when they realized their lives had ended.

Then, Shiloh thought, maybe that would be enough and he could be on about his business. But he did not draw the Springfield from the saddle boot. Instead he unhitched the horse and pulled it slowly and as quietly as possible through the bushes, cutting a trail that closed behind him through the the spring leaves.

For three quarters of a mile he led the chestnut through the trees in the dark. He heard the sound of running water before he saw it. And then he stepped in it. The stream had narrowed to the width of a small man's stride, but it was fairly deep and soaked his boot clean through.

He was a good mile downstream from the gunmen's camp. There was no clearing, but enough room for a man to lay down his bedroll. At first light, he would make his move.

6

SHILOH SLEPT LIGHTLY, waking to the sound of clattering birds before first light. His heart beat like a new drum in his chest, and for the briefest moment he wondered why. Above him the trees stood out in sharp detail against the star-crowded sky. A hint of blue already marked the coming dawn. The ground under his back was as soft as any featherbed. And the air was scented by pine and the dark rich earth, so that drawing in the first waking breath held its own pleasure.

So peaceful was the moment that he could not imagine himself rising. Then, feeling the weight of the Winchester across his stomach and the cold touch of the trigger under his finger, it came rushing back to him.

Now, as he rose, he brought the rifle to his side and stretched, throwing off the bedroll, which had offered little protection against the morning dew. He was soaked through to the bone. Even his boots, which he had not removed, were soaked. And then he remembered the night before and how he had stepped in the stream.

The chestnut was still tied where he had hitched it the

night before. The horse was awake as well, head bent to the stream, drinking.

Without dropping the rifle, he reached into the saddlebag and brought out a tough biscuit. It was about the only thing that wasn't damp. It was dry enough to gag on but filled his stomach.

For a long time Shiloh drank jaw to jaw with the chestnut. The water was so cold it set every tooth in his head aching. Then he saddled the chestnut, even as it continued to drink. He was careful to lift its front leg as he pulled the cinch tight, then brought its leg up again and gave the rig a final tightening. After securing the saddle, his saddlebags, Winchester, and Springfields to the beast, he was ready to go. It was nearly light, and he knew there wasn't much time.

Shiloh held the reins in one hand and the Winchester in the other as he led the chestnut back to the trail. He didn't have to get an up-close look to see that the gunmen's camp was empty. The fire was out and the horses were gone. The four men must have broke camp earlier, riding in darkness.

It was just getting to be first light, and the birds were now raising a racket above Shiloh's head. They were so loud that he barely heard the man behind him.

"Now ya just drop that rifle and get ya hands up," came the voice.

Without dropping the gun, Shiloh looked over his shoulder to see the man sitting astride a large roan. He was holding a Colt Lightning that pointed directly to the center of Shiloh's back.

"You got the wrong man, friend," Shiloh said, letting his finger wrap slowly around the trigger of the Winchester. "I'm just passing through."

"I bet, I just bet ya are," came the reply. "Now drop that gun or ya be dropping first."

"I don't know you, but I don't want no trouble," Shiloh tried. Out of the corner of his eye he could see the gunman climbing down from the roan. He slid off the saddle without so much as moving the gun an inch off Shiloh's back.

"I doan know ya neither, but I know that horse. Now drop that damned gun."

Turning slightly, Shiloh put a smile on his face and dropped the reins. "Listen, friend—"

But that's all he got out before the gunman fired a shot that kicked up a small spray of dirt a finger's length from Shiloh's boot. The chestnut took several nervous steps backward, but didn't bolt.

"Next one goes into yer back, friend," the gunman said. Then, with the last shot ringing in his ears, Shiloh heard the click of the Lightning's hammer falling into place.

Shiloh dropped the gun, tossing it lightly, trigger facing him, a few feet away.

"Now, s'pose you tell me where you happen to find that horse there?" the gunman asked, coming around Shiloh's side to pick up the rifle.

"Found him back a few miles, on the trail," Shiloh tried. "My own, she went lame. I had to shoot her."

The gunman was close now, Shiloh could feel him right at his ear. Then he could feel the Colt slip out of his holster. "Ya just sorta found it, wandering out here all by its lonesome, and ya out here with a lame dead horse. Ya be a lucky fella," the gunman sneered.

Now Shiloh could see him clearly. He was older than the boys, Malley and the other one, Horace. Shiloh figured him to be thirty, maybe a little younger. He wore a dirty gray hat, wide-brimmed with an open crown. He was heavyset, his small eyes set deep into his head. Even as he studied Shiloh, his mouth remained open as if he were about to say something, but forgot the words.

"I believe I never in my life hearda luck like that," he said as he gathered up the chestnut's reins and tossed the Winchester into the bushes. "But ya know, ya just ain't lucky no more."

"Why is that?" Shiloh asked, bringing his hands down slow.

"Keep them hands up! Ya ain't lucky on account a I gonna shoot ya," the gunman said.

"I got two thousand in gold in that saddlebag," Shiloh said, once again bringing his hands slowly down. "You can have it, all of it, if you let me go."

The gunman studied Shiloh for a moment; his mouth opened a notch wider. "My mamma didn't raise no fool. What's a tramp like ya doin' with two thousand?"

"Gonna give it to the first man I see today who don't shoot me," Shiloh answered.

The gunman made to reply, but curiosity had gotten the better of him. Keeping the Lightning trained on Shiloh, he walked around the chestnut and undid the saddlebag.

"Oh, damn, hot damn," he said, drawing out the Pinkerton sacks with the gold. "Goddamn! It is true!"

Now, with the chestnut and the roan between them, Shiloh dove for the Winchester. The gunman, dropping the sacks to the dirt, fired off a round from the Lightning that came so close Shiloh could feel it stream by his nose.

A small slope dropped away from the trail, and Shiloh rolled down it as he grabbed the Winchester and jacked a shell into its chamber, then fired off a shot in the direction of the gunman.

"Listen, pardner, ya got yerself a deal," the gunman called down the small gully. "I got the gold an' I doan want no trouble."

Shiloh answered with another shot from the Winchester. Then, scrambling through the rock-strewn side of the gully, he fired another.

Hearing the gunman's boots up on the trail and the sound of skittish horses, Shiloh figured the gunman to be putting the horses between himself and the gully. Even if Shiloh made it up to the edge of the incline and managed to get a shot off, he might hit one of the horses.

"Listen, pardner, ya jest stay down in that hole yonder and I be takin' yer leave, an' yer gold," the gunman called. "I assure ya, it was a true and mighty fine pleasure to make yer acquaintance."

It was now or never. Another second and Shiloh would be left without the gold or a horse. Digging a boot toe into the rocky slope, he sprang up and managed three scrambling steps to the top of the slope.

But even as he gained the top, Winchester already cocked as it came up across the sparse grass that lined the edge of the ditch, he could not see the gunman. Hearing the creak of leather, Shiloh slid the gun to his left and saw a worn boot, lifting to the stirrup on the other side of the road.

Shiloh fired off a round, missing the boot, but grazing the roan's belly. The big horse bucked the saddle, throwing the gunman out of the stirrup as it raised up on its hind legs. As Shiloh climbed from the gully, he watched the gunman being thrown backward from the mount. He came down hard on his back end as the roan vanished down the trail in a foaming-mouthed fit of fear.

For an instant, the gunman sat in a state of pain and shock, before reaching to his belt for the Lightning. But the pistol was not there. It lay a yard off in the dirt. With the outlaw's first move to the gun, Shiloh squeezed off a shot from the Winchester, firing from the hip as he approached the fallen rider. A little farther up the trail the chestnut worried at the bit in its mouth, edging its way back from the two men, but not likely to follow the roan.

"Ya think yer so all-fired smart, doan ya?" the gunman said with a bitter grin. "Ya must think yer jest 'bout the smartest man ever to step inta his pants in the mornin'."

"I have to ask myself just which one of us is sitting on his ass in the dirt," Shiloh replied, reaching down to pick up the gun.

"Then I gotta axe myself, whose two thousand in gold is heading hell-bent for Texas down that trail?"

Shiloh made for the chestnut, but even before he reached it, he knew the worst to be true. The gunman had transferred the gold to his own saddlebag, strapped to the roan, when Shiloh was on his stomach in the ditch.

Reaching into the chestnut's saddlebag, Shiloh came up with a handful of stale biscuits and .44 shells. When the gunman began to laugh, a deep-throated, satisfied laugh, Shiloh threw the biscuits and cartridges at him, scattering his food and ammunition along the trail. But it did not stop the laughter, if anything, it just added to the torturous mocking bray. "Goddamn, pardner," he managed to get out between gasping breaths. "I doan know where that hoss is headin' but it gonna get there twenty minutes 'fore its shadow!"

Shiloh turned a disbelieving gaze from the now-empty trail toward the gunman, raising the Winchester up slightly as he studied him. "How'd you like to get to hell twenty minutes before yours?"

"Oh, I doan believe I would much care for that, not atall," he said, a smile still spreading across his face. Then, reaching slowly out, he fetched up one of the tough biscuits and offered it to Shiloh. "Here, pardner, have a biscuit," he said, the gesture triggering a new burst of wheezing laughter.

7

THE GUNMAN WOULD not stop laughing. He laughed until tears flowed down his face, running small tracks in the trail dust from his eyes to his chin. He laughed until his belly heaved with pain and his breath would not come. And all the while he held out that damned biscuit.

Finally Shiloh could take it no longer. Walking up to the still sitting outlaw, he lowered the gun until it was inches from his face and cocked back the hammer. But the gunman continued to laugh, the sight of the rifle only stopping him momentarily until his entire body shook with a new wave of laughter.

"Looks like the only thing you got left, pardner, is biscuits an' bullets," he choked out as the spasms of mirth receded. "Biscuits and bullets!"

Shiloh kicked out violently at the sitting gunman. The toe of his boot catching the outlaw at the elbow and sending the biscuit flying. "I got myself a mind to put the next one right down your throat."

At this new threat the outlaw stopped laughing. Sitting

in the middle of the road, rubbing his wrist, he tried as best he could to catch his breath.

"Jest like my daddy usta say," the outlaw griped. "If it ain't funny, ya cain't laugh at it." And after saying his piece, the outlaw now seemed generally concerned with the cocked rifle leveled at his head.

"And what in hell is that supposed to mean?" Shiloh asked, stepping back and catching the chestnut's reins with one hand.

The gunman seemed to consider the question for a long time. The answer appeared genuinely important to him, seeing as the question was asked by a man with a Winchester to his head. "I be damned if'n I know, but that doan mean nothin'. Daddy weren't the sharpest tool in the shed, if'n ya know what I saying."

"Who are you people?" Shiloh asked, leading the chestnut around to his side, keeping his rifle pointed directly at the man's head.

This was a question the gunman didn't have to think about. He merely stared, silent, at the large black eye at the end of the Winchester. "It ain't no busy of yers," he replied finally.

"If you're with that outfit that shot my horse and tried to shoot me, then I suppose I got to make it my business."

"That weren't nothin', nothin' at all to do with ya," the man said, trying to get to his feet. "Or maybe it does?"

"You just sit yourself right back down there, friend," Shiloh instructed with a motion of the rifle. "You and me, we are gonna have ourselves a little talk."

"I toll ya, it ain't nothin', no concern a yers."

"You shot my horse, and you shot that boy, Malley," Shiloh replied, bending to pick up the cartridges and tough biscuits scattered across the ground. "Now, I don't know about Malley, but I was fond of that horse."

"I didn't shoot jackshit, pardner," the man answered, his gaze following the rifle's barrel.

"One of you people did, and I figure you all owe me," Shiloh replied, stuffing the cartridges in his pocket, and the biscuits in the chestnut's saddlebag.

"I doan owe ya nothin'."

"That boy, Horace, he's dead. Buried him with Malley, between the rocks, like a couple of new-marrieds."

The gunman seemed to think about this for a while. Then he looked around him and then back to Shiloh. "I say that's jest 'bout right. Jest 'bout what that little snot-nose had comin' to 'im."

Shiloh was growing tired of it. He was tired of all of it. The money was gone, and now he was out on the trail holding a rifle on a stranger and having to climb back on that damned chestnut. "I got myself a mind to shoot you, just like your people shot my horse. In the neck, that's where you got her, friend. And it wasn't a clean shot."

"I toll ya, and I gonna tell ya agin, I didn't shoot no horse and I didn't shoot no Malley. I'm jest plumb sorry 'bout that horse a yers, but I ain't sorry 'bout Malley, nor that little lyin' Horace. Now, ya cain shoot me, leave me be, or piss up a rope fer all I care."

Shiloh knew the gunman was serious. The man sitting at his feet didn't give a fiddler's damn if he died out on the trail with a bullet in his gut. He had no doubt killed enough men himself to know that death came to all men. Slow, fast, or sneaky, it caught up to everyone. And Shiloh himself knew that there were worse ways to die than an early morning bullet from a stranger. "Stand up, get on your feet."

"We goin' someplace?" the man asked, rising.

"Taking you into Silver Creek, see if you're worth anything to me."

"So that yer game, huh? If'n I knowed that gold in the saddlebag were blood money, I wouldn'ta touched it."

Retrieving a length of rope from the chestnut, Shiloh played out a few yards from the well-worn coil, enough to tie the man's hands. "You'd have stole it if it was dripping red."

The gunman was on his feet now, behind the chestnut, watching Shiloh begin a hitch in the length of rope. The Winchester was balanced lightly over Shiloh's arm, the trigger still within easy reach.

Shiloh never would have thought the gunman could move so fast. In a flash, he leapt toward the saddle boot and the Springfields. But even as Shiloh turned, finger sliding down toward the Winchester's trigger, the chestnut struck out. It kicked up its back hoof, bringing it off the ground in a blur of motion directed at the gunman.

The horse's hoof striking the outlaw made a sound like a hammer against a half-empty rain barrel. The blow sent the man flying up off his feet and then down with a soft thud. Now he lay in a crumpled heap behind the horse, who whinnied and stamped its front hooves with open-mouthed joy.

Shiloh cocked the Winchester and walked back to where the gunman had landed. He was still breathing, his face against the coarse dirt. "You all right, friend?" Shiloh asked, but the man made no reply. His eyes stared slightly downward, as if he had discovered the most fascinating thing in the world, lying in the dry dirt before him.

"You gonna make it?" Shiloh tried. When the man made no reply, Shiloh nudged him with his boot. This elicited only a slight sigh, so faint Shiloh could barely hear it over the sound of the excited chestnut's snorting.

Then Shiloh knelt to turn the outlaw over. He kept the Winchester trained on him, wary of tricks, but then he saw that the horse had caught him square in the head. The hoof had caved his skull in from temple to jaw. One dirt-covered eye sagged grotesquely out from the bloody mess. Brain, the color of stale bread, matted with bloodied hair was visible in the vague outline of the horse's hoof. It was as clean a blow as Shiloh had ever seen. The force of it had snapped the gunman's neck as neatly as a hangman's rope.

Rising from the body, Shiloh gave the chestnut a good long look before letting his gaze return to the dead man. "Laugh at that, you happy bastard," he said.

After picking up the remaining biscuits and cartridges and depositing them in the saddlebag, Shiloh knew that he had a choice to make. There was little doubt that the dead man was wanted, but was it worth the bother to haul him in to some small-town sheriff. It was a two-day ride to where the map said Silver Creek was, which meant it was more likely a three-day trip across rocky trails.

Shiloh studied the dead man as he would a side of Texas beef, trying to figure what price would be on his head. He put the number at somewhere between five and seven hundred. The gunman was too young and too stupid to be worth more than that. And then again, Shiloh was dead broke, except for two gold pieces he carried in his pocket.

As he stood studying the outlaw, Shiloh thought over his options. He'd been broke before, and he'd rode stirrup to stirrup with dead men. Neither choice was appealing. But on the whole, Shiloh finally decided he preferred broke to sharing a horse with a corpse.

"You wished that was me lying here with my head caved in, don't you?" Shiloh asked the horse as he went through the dead man's pockets. There wasn't any money, or rather none to speak of, but there was a map drawn in clumsy pencil on the back of a scrap of smudged white paper. It was traced or copied with care from a larger map, the lines running off the edges. A large X marked a position at the center. Halfway up toward the left corner were the initials S.C.

Studying the scrap of paper, Shiloh knew that it could be anywhere—Colorado, Utah, or California. The initials could have been anything, a person's name. But he knew they weren't. Studying the paper in the midmorning light, he guessed that S.C. could only be Silver Creek and that the clumsy X was near the spot he now stood, not half a mile from the gunmen's camp.

So, that was it. The gunmen had more than likely split up, riding on their own toward Silver Creek. Now all he needed to know was why. He knew that outlaws riding together took off on their own for many reasons, none of them good. Men being chased by a posse or the law broke off on their own. It was also the best way to ride into town if they were planning something in that town. And it was also the best way to ambush a lone rider.

Refolding the worn scrap of paper, Shiloh slipped it into his pants pocket. Then, half dragging and half carrying the dead outlaw, he brought him to the edge of the small gully and rolled him over the side. The body crashed awkwardly through the prickly bushes and over the stones, tumbling down the short rocky decline, before coming to rest against a small shrub bush.

The chestnut watched this procedure with keen interest, raising its head as the body rolled down the rocky slope. "I just bet you wished it were me," Shiloh said. "But I can't say I'm sorry to disappoint you."

Before mounting, Shiloh once again checked the chestnut's saddle, pulling the cinch tighter around its belly. Then he carefully inspected the crown, brow band, and throat latch, before taking the curb strap in a notch. The added pressure would make a normal horse more responsive, but it was a useless gesture, Shiloh knew, with this cold-mouthed, goose-rumped beast.

When Shiloh mounted the beast, he held firm on the cheek strap, turning the chestnut's head far around before climbing up into the saddle. As Shiloh tried pointing the horse up the trail, the chestnut proved more obstinate than before. Of course he could have let the horse have his head. He could follow the trail of the roan, hoping to find his gold. In a day or two he might find the roan, filling its belly by the side of a trail or lying on its side with a busted-up leg. It was possible.

The chestnut fought the bit, trying to turn back down the slope, toward the gold and the desert. Shiloh pulled up hard on the leather and turned the animal around. "You miserable piece of hide," Shiloh spat as he put the desert to his back. "You're just looking for a chance to get back down there."

Now before him was the steep climb of the hills, winding along a rocky trail. "But don't you know," Shiloh said, putting the spurs to the beast. "It ain't the money, and it never is the money until I start going hungry." The chestnut stamped furiously, rising slightly up on its front legs and sidestepping so close to the edge of the gully that Shiloh was sure the beast was trying to throw them both over out of spite. With a savage back-kick of his spurs, Shiloh set the horse on up the trail at a reluctant walk.

8

BY MIDAFTERNOON SHILOH and the chestnut had struck a grudging truce. It was as if a sudden sense of understanding had been reached between rider and horse. With the miles drifting by underfoot, each came to realize that the other was half mad.

Now they were riding on a narrow path. The larger trail that led up from the desert had forked north and south across the face of the hills. Following the tattered scrap of paper, Shiloh reined the chestnut south, on a trail hardly wider than a man's shoulders. It was thick and green now, with branches reaching out from either side, and the trail ahead obscured by sudden turns and trees.

Shiloh didn't like it. The trail was perfect for an ambush, a few yards on either side, a man with a rifle would not be seen. There were no clearings or signs of water, nothing that would let a man make a proper camp. More than likely it was an old Indian trail, which had not been used for months or even years.

These trails, he knew, crisscrossed the hills. If a man took a notion to, he could find a clearing and live for weeks or months by himself, feeding on the game that strayed close to his camp. Shiloh had ridden trails like these before. He had hunted men on them.

By dusk, Shiloh found water. A clearing marked a small spring no bigger than the mouth of a water barrel. Its muddy banks overflowed across smooth stones and down a gentle incline into the green of the hills.

Without dismounting, Shiloh let the chestnut drink. The horse lapped at the water thirstily, but not desperate, as if it expected water. Then Shiloh climbed down, led the horse to a far corner of the small clearing, and knelt beside the water, cupping his hands to drink and wash his face in the clear, flowing spring.

It was quiet, not the humming silence of the desert that filled a man's brain with murderous thoughts or drove him to madness, but the peaceful quiet found among trees. The sounds of the small breezes through branches thick with leaves and the wet trickle of the water across the rocks whispered their message. *Here is life and those things man needs for life. You may feast here, drink the water, kill what food you require, and let your eyes rest on the green that surrounds you. This is what man requires and nothing more.*

Laying his hat beside him by the spring, Shiloh sent his eyes wandering over the small clearing. The chestnut was pulling small leaves from a low bush and chewing them contentedly around the cool metal of the bit. And he knew, as he had discovered a hundred times before in such places, that the singing quiet of this solitude was not what he hungered for. Surely it had seemed like that at times. In the smoke-clouded air of saloons and the jostling ride of Concord stages, he had fairly ached for such a place. He had longed for it as he had never wanted any woman or any whiskey.

Though now that he sat by the water, resting on the cool earth and smelling the pine-scented air, he knew it to be a trick. The desert at least had taken away the dreams. But here the dead would follow him. The fear would return to haunt him while he slept. Because Shiloh knew that wherever a man finds his peace, it's there that fear will find him. Give a man a million dollars in a granite bank with brass doors and he'll worry over pennies. Put a beautiful woman in his bed and he'll fret over her love. Offer him a merciful God and he'll find sin. And bring him deliverance from death and hell will haunt him to the grave.

That night, hell came to Shiloh's camp. As the fire burned to white ash and the stars shone close through the cool air, he once again dreamed of the dead. They came back to him from that battlefield in Tennessee, buddies and butternuts, their faces torn and bleeding from grapeshot and bullets. Their uniforms, muddied from the spring rain, hung in rags against their corpse bodies. Each one stared at him with eyes that burned with hate and greedy envy. Those whose eyes had been torn from their heads came to him with contorted fingers, mouths twisting in damning curses beneath the empty bloody sockets.

It was a vision from hell that damned Shiloh. And he knew that they were judging him. Once they had been good men and now they were dead. Once they had laughed and ate and cried and now they were buried together in shallow graves dug into the clay, wearily by those under orders. Once they had loved and been loved, and now they were no longer mourned, for the living cannot stand the pain of loss forever. Now their foreshortened lives were forever bound with that which had been their demise; "Joby died at Shiloh, fighting for the Union" or "Yankees killed Wayne in '62."

Years later, that is what they had become, not even memories of the men they were by those who knew them, loved them. And what was it that Shiloh had become, that is what they begged to know. Each dead face asked the same question: "What is it that you have done with the life we were robbed of?"

And Shiloh knew. As clearly as he knew that he was dreaming, he knew the damning answer. He was a hunter of men, alone and without the comforts the living crave. An outcast. He did not yearn and was perhaps even unfit for that which is every man's right, a wife, a child, and a home.

When he woke, Shiloh rose in darkness, shivering from clothes soaked through with sweat. From across the clearing, the chestnut eyed him suspiciously. He feared that the horse had smelled the terror pouring from him as he slept. Often, he knew, he screamed or moaned in his sleep, and it was this that had most likely spooked the horse.

Relighting the fire, Shiloh built it up to a waist-high blaze. Then he stripped down buck naked and changed into fresh clothes. They smelled of horse and sweat, but they were dry.

For a long time he watched the fire burn down. Then he rolled himself a smoke, laying the Gold Flake tobacco neatly into the paper, portioning it out with a careful finger before licking the paper and rolling the fixings into a neat quirly. He lit the thin paper tube with a twig from the fire, remembering that he had seen one of the gunmen do the same two days ago.

The thin blue line of smoke rose lazily in the cool air. The slight breeze had died and now dawn was coming. It would be full light soon. He was not hungry, at least not for the biscuits that were left in the saddlebag. Coffee would have been welcome, but he had none. The gunman had packed Shiloh's food, like the gold, on the roan.

It was then that Shiloh saw the smoke, rising from below in a white line just beyond the treetops. He studied it as if he had never seen smoke before. It was the smoke of a cook fire, he was certain. The camp was a good two miles ahead of him and perhaps another mile downward.

There was a chance that it was the other gunmen, then, too, the fire may have been a prospector trying his luck farther up in the hills or a government survey man taking measurements for a map. Whoever had lit the fire, there was an excellent chance that they were better equipped than Shiloh. Perhaps they had coffee or maybe they had seen the gunmen.

Shiloh saddled the chestnut carefully, lifting its front leg to tighten the cinch, then again just to make certain, as he pulled the buckle tight. Whatever was wrong with the beast, Shiloh was now convinced that the animal wasn't a jughead. There was a world of difference, he knew, between a horse that was dumb and one that was just plain mean. Either one might kill you, but at least a man had a chance when he climbed on a mean-spirited animal.

Pulling hard on the reins to bring the chestnut back on the trail, Shiloh soon found a path that led down toward where he had seen the fire. The ride would be longer than he had first thought, maybe half a day. And if the men at the camp were traveling in anything that looked like a hurry, they would be long gone by the time Shiloh arrived.

Soon it was daylight, and the last gray wisps of smoke vanished from the sky, carried off slowly by the small breeze, which once again began to blow down from the mountain. As the last traces of the cook fire vanished, Shiloh came on the creek. It was barely a trickle, no wider than a man's arm, but it was heading in the same direction as Shiloh. So he pulled off the trail and followed it.

There, in the rocky streambed, through the swift-running water, he saw the marks. They were the same as the tracks he had followed two days before, when he tracked the gunmen to their camp. Now, he noticed, they were less careful about covering their trail. More than likely, they assumed that their good-humored friend had already disposed of the problem who was dogging their trail.

Several times the chestnut slipped on the slick rocks but regained its footing quickly. The trail Shiloh now rode was not cut through the trees by man, but rather by water, and had followed its own course. The stream fell rapidly from the hills, over flat rocks and through grown-over shrubs, but the chestnut followed it nicely, several times picking its way around a fallen tree or large stone to find its own way back to the water. So concerned was the chestnut with following the rocky trail, that it forgot to disobey Shiloh's commands at the reins.

When Shiloh finally arrived at the empty camp the sun was up. There had been coffee; the grounds, still wet, lay across the small bed of ash. The moist, chewed ends of two cigars lay nearby, next to an empty whiskey bottle.

Without climbing down from the chestnut, Shiloh inspected the camp. He could see boot prints of four riders and pickets for three horses staked at one end of the camp. Like the camp he had seen by the overhang, it was a good place to rest for men on the run. A jagged wall of rock protected one side, while the two trails leading in were clearly visible.

Shiloh swiveled in the saddle and took one more look at the campsite, noting that the three sets of tracks followed one trail down the mountain. "Well, looks like we're about a day late and a dollar short," he whispered to the chestnut.

In response the horse pissed a long, splashing stream over the empty liquor bottle and cigar butts.

9

"ONE DAY, THEY are going to find all them liquor bottles and spent shells, just like arrowheads," Shiloh told the chestnut. "And do you know what they are gonna say?"

The horse made no reply.

"Well, they are gonna say, 'These men drank too damn much.' And then they are gonna say, 'With all that drinking, it is surely a miracle if any of them could shoot straight enough to kill another.' " The chestnut greeted Shiloh's speculation with silence.

It was a glorious day by anyone's reckoning. The night fears had long left Shiloh, and as he followed the gunmen's trail, not even this grim task could keep his mood completely dark.

They were heading southwest now, the trail that Shiloh had followed from the gunmen's camp had joined a wider trail. This new trail was overlaid with a sun-dappled canopy of new spring leaves.

It amazed Shiloh that a two-day ride from the desert could put him in such a place. On higher ground, he knew, the desert would be visible. There was a place on the

California-Nevada border he had heard of, where a man could climb for a day and look out over snow-covered valleys to the north, then turn in his tracks and see the flat expanse of desert to the east.

Pulling the crude map from his pocket, Shiloh realized that this was the proper trail toward Silver Creek. In a few miles, the gunmen's tracks were joined, then lost in the repeated cut of wagon wheels and the smaller prints of mules drawn in a team. This new trail, Shiloh could see, was a well-traveled road. The wagon cuts were deep, the work of full loads of timber, ore, and supplies.

There was something unsettling about it all for Shiloh. He had been alone for a month or more. His only exchange had been with those who tried to kill him. Now, once again, he was entering the world of men. It was as strange and foreboding as foreign country. Quite by surprise, he felt himself ambushed by the old longings, a soft bed, an indoor fire, and the taste of whiskey.

It was these thoughts now, and not the gunmen, that urged Shiloh along as he put the rowels to the chestnut's sides. After not missing the comforts of town for a month, suddenly he could not wait.

Then he heard the shots. There were two of them, so close together they could have been mistaken for a single blast.

Pulling up hard on the chestnut, Shiloh stopped in the center of the trail and waited. But no other shots followed. He was at a turn, banked by a wall of rock on one side and a drop on the other.

It might have been hunters, a pair of tin pans turning from their golden dreams to some game. Though Shiloh knew, instinctively, that this was not the case. Nudging the chestnut to a slow walk, Shiloh turned a wide bend and followed the trail that now sloped down. He was getting close now, he could feel it. The shots could not have been more than a half mile ahead.

When he was almost to the place where he thought the shots came from, Shiloh pulled the Winchester from its saddle boot and put the spurs to the horse. As he came to the next turn in the trail, he kept close to the trees, the cocked rifle waiting at his side.

Then he saw them. He took the scene in with a glance, seeing every part of it as clear as a picture. It was as if the gunmen were old friends by now; even with the pieces of sack tied to their faces, he recognized the one who had lit the fire and fixed the coffee two nights back. But he wasn't holding a coffeepot now. He was holding a shotgun in one hand and a pistol in the other, and both were leveled at the shotgun messenger of the Fargo stage.

There were four of them and three horses. One of them was on the ground, reaching up to the stage's front boot for the treasure box. Another held the harness of the lead horses with one hand and his reins and a pistol in the other. The six-horse team stamped and back-stepped as the driver struggled and cursed, trying to calm them as another outlaw held the ten gauge trained on him.

The fourth sat atop his horse, pistol resting along his leg easily as he barked orders. "Just get the damned box down. Don't be afraid of bustin' the damned thing, there's gold, not glass in it." Shiloh recognized the man giving orders as the man who had walked away from the horses by his ragged, dirt-brown hat.

"Ya heard him. Git on with it!" the man holding the team hollered.

Shiloh could hear the voice clearly from where he sat, barely concealed from the outlaws. It was the voice that had called him a dead man back in the desert.

As Shiloh watched, the outlaw dropped the box from

the coach, splitting open its side, but not spilling its contents. Without taking either the pistol or the shotgun messenger's own weapon off the man, he smashed in one side of the wooden container with a savage stamp of his boot heel, splitting it neatly along the new-painted script letters that read "Wells, Fargo."

Shiloh made his choice fast. Bringing the Winchester up to his shoulder, he squeezed a shot off at the outlaw holding the bridle of the lead horse.

It hit the outlaw like the wrath of God, first turning him in the saddle as the .44 slug bored into his shoulder, then yanking the lead horses' bridle from his hand as he fell to the ground.

As the panicked horses thrust forward, the outlaw standing on the board with the shotgun to the driver's head was thrown back, discharging the gun and further panicking the team. In an instant, the wagon and its six horses were between Shiloh and the two remaining outlaws.

"Come on, you bastard idiot! Kill that sonofabitch," the outlaw with the pistol yelled to his comrade on the ground, who had kicked the box and was now desperate to get at the stolen treasure and retreat. "Kill him! Kill him!"

Using the Fargo wagon as cover, Shiloh spurred his horse forward, managing to squeeze off four more rounds toward the outlaws. They fired back as one, their slugs pounding into the wagon's side and nicking one of the horses, who trampled his way forward in pain.

The three of them were on their feet now, guns out and shooting. One of the bullets hit the driver, tossing him from the box. As the reins fell free, the team thundered down the trail, two wheels rising up from the dusty road as the stampeding team managed the curve.

Digging the spurs in, Shiloh pulled the chestnut around

and took shelter behind the turn in the road. When he had enough cover, he stepped down from the chestnut and tied the quivering beast to a small pine. There was a break in the rocks formed by a trickle of a stream, and Shiloh scampered up it, boots slipping on the slick surface. If he could gain the higher ground, then he would have a chance against the outlaws.

He had three of them to worry about now. The fourth lay in the road bleeding, he wouldn't be much good with a bullet in his shoulder.

Shiloh stalked up the hill silently, carefully charting a course through the thick brush toward the lip of the rock wall. When he heard the horses, he moved quickly, finally reaching the edge panting, Winchester to his shoulder. But the outlaws were gone. The Fargo box lay in a broken heap in the center of the road, among a dozen gleeming empty shell casings. A dark stain of blood marked where the one gunman had fallen with Shiloh's bullet in his shoulder.

Walking back to the chestnut, Shiloh found it drinking from a ditch that marked the end of the shallow stream. The Fargo driver lay dead a few feet away. His arm was bent back at an impossible angle, like a sideshow act.

Shiloh studied the dead coach driver without kneeling to the dead man. Then he knelt beside the horse and drank jaw to jaw with it for a long time, splashing handfuls of the icy water onto his face before getting to his feet.

Wearily Shiloh slipped the Winchester into the boot and climbed back on the horse. Then he turned the animal around and followed the crooked tracks of the Concord.

He didn't have a long ride. The coach went off the road a quarter mile down it. It lay on its side spread out across the sharp incline, the six-horse team tangled before it in a gasping and tortured hill of horse flesh. The animals that were still alive cried out in pain or panic or both as they strained against the leather harness.

Hitching the chestnut, Shiloh half slid, half climbed down the hill. The shotgun messenger was dead, crushed beneath the front of the wagon, its weight pressing the once big man's chest down so that it was impossibly thin. The thick reins lay snakelike, just out of reach from the dead man's hands.

Approaching the horses, Shiloh pulled the Sheffield bowie from his back sheath and studied the grisly scene. The animals' heaving chests moved in quick, panicked breaths. From beneath the two horses that landed on top came a gasping death rattle of the other four in a chorus of animal pain.

Slowly moving among the wounded animals, Shiloh cut the guide lines with the knife, whispering softly to the animals as he worked. When the lines were cut, he pulled first on one horse's bridle, trying to coax him up. The horse made a brave attempt to move, then lay back down gasping on its side. Its ribs were broken.

The next horse rose on shaky legs. It snorted blood over Shiloh's shirt, then fell to its knees, and rose again, its legs shaking under it. Shiloh hitched the animal to a tree with a length of cut leather and fired five bullets into the ears of the other dying animals.

10

IT WAS NOT a pleasant ride to Silver Creek. Shiloh had wrapped the bodies of the shotgun messenger and driver with a length of canvas from the Concord and tied them to the only survivor of the crash, which he led behind the chestnut on a length of leather coach rein.

They had traveled less than two miles when he realized the stage horse was in trouble. At first the animal seemed only reluctant, pausing every fifty yards or so. Then she began to stumble, her front legs buckling under her as she struggled to continue on. When Shiloh heard the animal's wet, gasping breathing, he knew the horse would not reach town. The poor beast had hurt something bad on her insides.

It took another mile for the horse to die. But it went out like a faithful Wells, Fargo employee. Shiloh could say that much. If anyone on the company's payroll deserved a silver watch and their sketch in the paper, it was that horse. Watching the animal on the ground, still struggling to stand under the burden of the two dead men, Shiloh gave her the next best thing, a bullet in the ear.

With the Fargo horse gone, Shiloh untied the two dead men and dragged their bodies to the side of the trail. It was a dry, rocky spot. Then he double-tied the canvas tight, wrapping the coach rein around the canvas. Using his knife, Shiloh carved a slash into the largest tree. This done, he remounted the chestnut and made for town.

When he finally saw Silver Creek, it was more than he expected. In fact, it was a proper town, built right against the mountains. It appeared to have more than two dozen buildings and a small mining operation. As Shiloh rode down from the hills, he wondered what kind of reception he would receive. Riding into town with dead outlaws would raise a stir, but coming in with the news of a stage robbery and two valued employees of Wells, Fargo & Company laid out dead on the trail and trussed up like hogs would no doubt require some explaining.

It was going on dusk when Shiloh approached town. Mercifully, the sheriff's office was one of the first buildings he saw. It was next to the Fargo office.

No sooner had Shiloh hitched his horse to the post than the Fargo agent was out of his office on the boards, watching. He was a small, round man wearing a green eyeshade, spectacles, and a neatly barbered set of muttonchops. The sleeves of his white shirt were held up by a pair of garters. A large gold watch chain spanned his ample belly across a black vest.

"Cain't hitch yer hoss there, friend," the Fargo man said. "Stage only at that post, be here soon, too."

"Stage isn't coming in on time today," Shiloh replied. "The sheriff in?"

"What you mean, not on time," came the outraged response. "Why I would bet my last . . ."

"The stage was held up, your driver and shotgun are

dead up in the hills,'' Shiloh said, taking a step toward the law's office.

''Held up? When? Where?'' the Fargo man asked, his whiskers quivering at the prospect. ''Son, you best go see the sheriff.''

Shiloh stopped with one foot in the street, the other resting on the step to the sheriff's office. ''That's just what I'm aiming to do,'' he said, looking the Fargo man in the eye.

''Well, you won't find 'im there,'' came the answer as the little man blocked Shiloh's way. ''No, sir, but you'd better see the sheriff directly.''

''And just where do you suppose he is?''

''He's workin' over at the saloon, Native Son,'' the Fargo man stammered. ''Cain't miss 'im.''

Shiloh made his way across the street to the saloon, the Fargo man yapping at his heels like a pup. They were both greeted at the batwings by the inviting smell of liquor, loud laughter, and a prominent, meticulously lettered sign beside the double-wide door that began with the familiar poem:

The miners came in 'forty-nine,
The whores in 'fifty-one,
They rolled upon the barroom floor,
And made the Native Son.

WELCOME ALL
Best Drinking Whiskies,
Finest Stepping Young Ladies
&
Smoothest Smoking Cigars
FARO, POKER, AND OTHER
GENTLEMANLY GAMES

OF SKILL AND CHANCE PROVIDED COURTESY OF B. Z. WALKER, SHERIFF

The sheriff was sitting on a velvet-cushioned chair behind a faro layout. He wore a spotless broadcloth coat over an embroidered white shirt. The diamond stickpin that held his blue tie around his throat caught the lamp light from across the room. Next to him stood the strangest faro casekeeper that Shiloh had ever seen; a young boy with blond, nearly white hair, wearing a pair of ragged pants and a worn coat, nearly identical to the sheriff's.

Shiloh studied the lawman as three players bucked the tiger without success. All the while, the sheriff kept up a friendly patter of conversation, jokes, and poems, which held the losers to the table.

Shiloh pegged him for an experienced gambler, but also the kind of man who would good-naturedly be the chief judge in the church baking contest just as easily as he'd quiet a saloon with his word and reputation.

"No, I expect that you ain't deliverin' me any good news today, Smitty," the sheriff said, pushing the faro box away from him and nodding to the players to show that the game was finished. His hair was a sun-bleached color of dirty blond, not unlike Shiloh's, though better barbered. "Who might yer friend be?"

"Says somebody's robbed the stage," the little man stammered. "Told 'im ta talk to ya."

"No, sir, not very pleasant news," Shiloh replied as the sheriff pushed back the cushioned chair and stood. He was a tall man, who met Shiloh's gaze head on. "They robbed the Fargo wagon, killed the driver and guard."

"And who might you be?" the sheriff asked with a hint

of Scotch in his voice. ''If you're one of the bandits, it would make my job a bit easier.''

''No, I wasn't with them,'' Shiloh said as he watched the sheriff move around from the table.

''Then I guess we best go back to my office and talk it over,'' the lawman said, putting on the black, low-brimmed hat the boy held for him.

The sheriff didn't waste time. With a nod to the watchful bartender, they were soon walking briskly out of the saloon. The young boy, who Shiloh now noticed was barefoot, ran ahead of them as the sheriff, Shiloh, and the Fargo man made their way across the boards and into the street. They paused only once as the sheriff tipped his hat graciously in a half bow to a pair of ladies who passed, under the lace-fringed cover of parasols.

Shiloh watched the women's progress for a moment, then turned back to the sheriff. ''There were four of them, I've been dogging them for the better part of a week.''

''Smitty, is the stage late, like this gent says it is?'' the sheriff asked the small man.

''Yes, sir, going on an hour an' a half now,'' came the answer.

When they reached the sheriff's office, the lawman turned again to Shiloh. ''Now then, that is all very nice, but it don't answer my question, which I believe was who are you?''

''Shiloh, that's what they call me.''

''Now then, Mr. Shiloh, just what is your business with these men you say shot up the stage?''

''I've been trailing them for the better part of a week,'' Shiloh offered again. ''They shot a boy I found wandering in the desert, had his throat slit. When they tried it on me I started following them.''

"You must be a brave man, Mr. Shiloh, following four men, killers, by your lonesome."

"There were six of them back when I first met up with them."

The sheriff considered Shiloh for a long moment, his hand resting lightly on the handle of his sidearm. "Mister, I believe that you are fixin' to tell me a long story."

"Yes, sir," Shiloh replied, moving toward the office door, helped along by the sheriff's hand that rested friendly on his back.

"In that case, I would be obliged if you stepped in here and told it," he said with a broad gambler's smile. "And, Smitty, get on the telegraph and see if that stage left on time. It ain't that I'm calling you a liar, but it will give Smitty here something to do while we talk."

Without argument, the small man came off the porch and trotted down the street.

"Now, about that story you were fixin' on telling me?" the sheriff asked, pushing his hat high on his head.

And with that Shiloh stepped into the cool darkness of the lawman's office, aware that while one of the sheriff's hands eased him into the office, the other rested lightly on the pistol at his hip.

"What I wanna know is who is that sumbitch?" the small man asked.

There were four of them, squatting around a small fire. Through the trees they could just about make out the dark outline of Silver Creek. The town, with its three saloons and two whorehouses, lay just below them. The first evening's lights were coming to life up and down the short main street of the town.

"What business he got with us, anyhow, Marcus?" the tallest of the lot asked. "We didn't do nothin' to him."

"Ya must mean nothin' aside from tryin' to shoot him like that Malley. Is that the kinda nothin' ya mean?" the man who spoke was smaller and older, yet the family resemblance between him and the tall one was unmistakable.

"I jest wanta git ta town," a third chimed in. He was a big, soft-featured man. Though his face was deeply scarred from scarlet fever, it was his eyes that held a stranger's attention. They were yellow, like a cat's. Now he was stripped to his long underwear from the waist up. A bloodied rag was tied against his shoulder. "A gent in Creed, half Ingin bar-dog, said they got this Frenchie gal, and she done it with the King a Spain."

"I doan believe it, Clay," the small man said. "I jest doan."

"What, that she done it with the King a Spain?" came the hurt reply.

"No, jest that there's a half Indian barkeep in Creed."

"If you boys are done foolin'," the fourth man spoke up. "We have got ourselves a genuine problem here." With his first words, the other three gave him their full attention. He wasn't the biggest of the lot, but he was the smartest and the others knew it.

"Clay, you hurting from that shoulder?"

"I ain't hurt 'nuf not to see that Frenchie gal." The big man grinned. Then seeing that the other did not smile back, he added, "I think it stopped bleedin', Sam. Ya fixed it up real good."

"Now, that's good, real good," the leader replied. "We can't have you riding into town bleeding like a stuck pig, can we?"

A general sigh of relief passed through the three others, for they knew that it was Sam who would have the final word of whether they rode into Silver Creek, or just kept riding. And none of them was too eager to stay on the trail; not when what they could take out of the town's bank, saloon, and post office would set them up nice.

"When do we git our money?" the big one, Randy, asked, already figuring on ways to spend it.

"I say, when do we split it?" the smaller one, Marcus, chimed in.

"No reason we can't count it up now?" Sam replied. "You don't see any reason to object, do you, Clay?"

"Hell no!" the big man answered quickly, readjusting the bloody covering of the bandage.

"Now you wouldn't bleed on it, Clay?" Sam persisted as he rose to retrieve the stolen Fargo money from a saddlebag that lay behind him.

"No, I ain't gonna bleed on it, Sam."

The two brothers, Marcus and Randy, watched this exchange impatiently. Both knew that Clayton Burrows was a half-wit. But he was loyal to Sam, no matter what kind of teasing he took from the man. And each remembered too well the little display Sam had put on in a saloon in San Francisco.

Loading his gun in plain view, Sam then handed it to Clay. "Put it in your mouth," he had said with a smile.

And Clay stuck the business end of the Lightning's barrel into his mouth like it was a chunk of sirloin.

"Do you trust me, Clay?" Sam then asked.

The half-wit motioned his head up and down as a barroom full of people watched, gaping.

"If you trust me, then pull the trigger," Sam said, smiling. "It's a joke, Clay. A trick."

The big man pulled back on the trigger, all the time looking at Sam, who nodded with cool reassurance.

When the trigger clicked into place, Sam moved, jamming his hand down fast, so that the hammer fell on the soft wedge of skin between his thumb and forefinger. Then, ever so gently, he took the gun away from the big man.

"Here, Clay, buy yourself a drink on me," he then said and gave Clay a double eagle.

Sam's exhibition had stuck with the two brothers ever since, just as Sam Follard had intended that it should. For they knew that Clay would do Sam's bidding, no matter if it meant risking his own life in the process.

"Now, I don't want you boys worrying about that blond jasper no more," Sam said as he counted out the Wells, Fargo money. "He's just some poor-luck tramp who stumbled into something that isn't none of his concern."

"Horace is dead," Randy said, recounting his small pile of coins and admiring the warm glow the fire lent to the gold. "And we ain't seen Lester since we . . ."

"I don't want you boys worrying about him," Sam said, suddenly stopping his count. "Clay, you saw that jasper, remember?"

"I seen 'im, out in the desert, I saw 'im," the big man replied.

"Well, if you see him again," Sam said, his voice suddenly turning low and serious, "shoot him. You understand? We, all of us, are counting on you."

"I see 'im again I shoot 'im," Clay said, bringing his old Army Colt from its place in his belt. "I see 'im agin he a dead man."

"Clay, he was a dead man when he stuck his nose in our business," Sam said, patting the big man on his good shoulder. "You, well, you are just finishing the job."

Sam Follard continued to count money out to the three others, systematically short-counting Clay and talking all the while. But he did not mention his encounter with Shiloh in the rocks, back near the desert. He dared not mention how luck had sent his glance up to the rocks to see the unknown man leveling the sights of a Springfield on him. And how only split-second cunning had saved him. The brothers were now riding double because he fell alseep during his watch. It wouldn't do to lose their respect; besides, they had already accepted the story about the horses being spooked by a rattler as willingly as a child accepts a fairy tale.

11

SILVER CREEK'S LAWMAN had been a smooth customer, Shiloh would offer that much about him. No sooner had the two men walked through the door than Shiloh noticed the boy, the casekeeper from the Native Son and probably not any older than sixteen, sitting in a chair by the double cell, with a hog-leg pointed at Shiloh's belly.

With a motion of his hand, the sheriff made the introductions. "This here is Amos. And, Amos, this is Mr. Shiloh. He's gonna be spending a few days with us 'til I figure out what's what."

The boy nodded agreeably, without lowering the big pistol.

"Mr. Shiloh, I would surely be obliged if you'd hand over that gun," the sheriff asked, polite as a preacher passing the collection plate. "And that sticker, too. The one strapped on behind."

The sheriff was still smiling when Shiloh unbuckled the belt and offered it to the sheriff. His smile widened a notch as he took the knife and sheath. "Don't worry yourself about them. They'll be safe as in a bank, what with Amos looking after them."

"I got a saddle and roll on that chestnut," Shiloh said as the sheriff opened the iron door to the cell. "The repeater's mine, but I took two Springfields from the men that took the stage."

The sheriff, closing the door behind Shiloh, smiled again. "Don't you worry 'bout them. I'll have Smitty fetch back the roll, to make you feel at home, and Amos'll look after that rifle."

"How long?" Shiloh asked, looking around the small cell, then noticing a sleeping Mexican on a bunk at the far corner.

"Oh, two days, maybe less," the sheriff replied. "Depending on how fast I can get the telegraph operator sober enough to send word. I truly appreciate your cooperating and all. Supper's already been served and eaten, but I think there's a little peach cobbler left and some coffee if you're hungry. Little gal over at the cafe makes it just right."

And with that the sheriff hung the cell's keys on a hook and made to leave the room. It was the slickest job that Shiloh had ever seen of getting a man behind bars. "Sheriff! Hey, Sheriff, what do I call you anyway?" Shiloh yelled through the bars.

The sheriff's head popped around the doorway with a wide grin. "Bernard Zechariah Walker, at your service. Folks just mostly call me B.Z. though. Now you just sit tight, and I'll see about that cobbler."

The boy, Amos, with the hog-leg did not speak. Standing in front of the cell, he considered Shiloh for a moment, then moved back away from the bars and sat himself down in a slat-backed chair, picked up a newspaper and began to read. The pistol rested comfortably in his lap.

"Eh, amigo, don you worry, B.Z., he a good man,"

the Mexican said from the cot. "Fair lawman you ever see, amigo. And that coobler, it good."

The Mexican spoke moving his lips slightly and opening only one eye. The one half-opened eye studied Shiloh as he moved away from the bars.

"How long you been here?" Shiloh asked.

"One day, maybe two, *eee-chinga*, drunk so drunk tha filthy *puta* of a wife, she call B.Z. She come take me home soon, you teek thees cot, beast one."

"I'm obliged," Shiloh said. But the Mexican did not hear him, he was already back to sleep.

"Son, hey, son," Shiloh called to the boy reading the paper. "I would be obliged for a drink of water."

The young boy looked over lazily at Shiloh, put down the paper, and picked up the pistol. After a moment of study, he walked outside and came back with a tin cup of water.

Shiloh reached through the bars to take the cup, but the boy shook his head and motioned him back against the wall with his free hand.

When Shiloh was against the far wall, the boy balanced the cup on a cross bar and stepped back away. He went through the entire routine very deliberately and without speaking.

Shiloh drained the cup in a swallow, the cool water clearing away some of the trail's dust. Then he replaced the cup on a cross bar, but the boy made no move to retrieve it.

The sheriff came back soon after that. He was carrying a tray covered with a blue-checkered cloth in one hand and a coffeepot in the other. When he made for Shiloh's cell, the boy stood up from his chair and once again leveled the pistol at Shiloh's stomach.

The sheriff smiled the same social grin as he watched

Amos take the keys down from their place on the wall. "Now, if you just move back from that door a mite, I can serve supper," the sheriff said.

Shiloh stepped back from the door, but even against the far wall he could smell the cobbler. The door was opened only long enough for the sheriff to set the tray and coffee down. "There you go, supper. There was stew, but that's gone. I put some carrots on there, and the coffee is fresh," the sheriff said as pleasantly as any hotel waiter. "Now, suppose you tell me about that horse."

"Not much to tell," Shiloh replied, lifting the blue-checkered napkin off the tray. A steaming cobbler and six carrots sat there and a spoon sat across its worn wood surface. The crust of the cobbler looked flaky brown, just the way Shiloh liked it. "Not much to tell. When they shot mine, I just sorta took it."

"Seems like someone took it 'fore you," the sheriff said. "You wouldn't know nothin' 'bout that brand?"

"Just that someone was at it before I found it," Shiloh said, still kneeling beside the steaming cobbler.

"And 'bout them bullet holes in the saddle?"

Shiloh dug a spoon into the cobbler and brought the steaming mound to his mouth. It was delicious. "That's my saddle. Those holes are where they shot it up."

The sheriff pulled a chair up to the bars from behind his desk, then sat with the back of the chair under his chin. He was still smiling as he watched Shiloh devour the cobbler and wash it down with coffee. "I wasn't lyin' to you 'bout that cobbler, was I?"

"No, sir, it's the best I had in a spell," Shiloh said, licking the thick spoon and then his fingers.

"I was tellin' you the hundred percent truth about it. Now, suppose you tell me the truth 'bout what happened to you out there."

And Shiloh did. He told him all of it, from finding Malley in the desert, to how he shot the other one, Horace, and how the outlaw was kicked in the head. As Shiloh talked, Amos moved quietly around the office lighting the lamps.

And the sheriff, he didn't listen like other lawmen Shiloh had met. He smiled and nodded just as pleasant as could be. Even when Shiloh's tale became farfetched, the sheriff only raised an eyebrow.

Finally, when Shiloh was finished, the lawman raised himself up out of the chair and stretched. "Well, sir, that sure is a story. A reg'lar adventure you had yourself."

"Then you believe me?" Shiloh asked, sipping a cup of cold coffee to ease his now dry throat.

"I ain't sayin' I believe you," the sheriff confessed as he walked back to his desk. "But I ain't callin' you a liar, neither. What I want is for you to sit in there and not cause trouble 'til I get my telegraph answers back from that town up north you say you jest visited, what is it, Splendid? Then there's Wells, Fargo, the federal marshal's office, and the Pinkertons. And that may take a spell."

Near midnight a plump Mexican woman came into the sheriff's office. The boy seemed to know what she wanted, and he quickly and wordlessly went to the desk and picked up the pistol.

As the Mexican woman watched, the boy roused Shiloh from his bedroll on the top bunk and made him stand against the wall. Then, very carefully, he opened the gate and let the woman into the cell.

She woke the Mexican up with a string of rapid Spanish and two-handed nudgings, then half carried and half pushed him out through the cell's door.

"Adios, amigo, that bunk, ees yours now," the sleepy Mexican called over his shoulder.

"Good-bye, *compadre*," Shiloh answered.

The boy locked the cell with a careful businesslike manner and returned to the desk and to reading the newspaper.

"Hey, boy!" Shiloh called through the bars. "Amos! You figure the sheriff'll let me out of here soon?"

The boy looked up from his paper, turned his head toward Shiloh, and shrugged.

"Amos! You like to play checkers?" Shiloh tried. He had noticed a checkerboard and cigar box full of pieces on the sheriff's desk. "Bet I could whup you in checkers!"

The boy raised his head again and studied Shiloh for a long time. Finally, he returned to his reading, deciding not to take Shiloh up on the challenge. Shiloh noticed that he read very slowly, moving his finger across the type.

Sometime later the sheriff returned, his boots sounding their way loudly over the boards and through the office door. Shiloh was half asleep on the cot. The sheriff said something to the boy and then the door closed. By that time Shiloh could feel himself falling full asleep.

Shiloh fell into sleep easily, dropping off into the darkness all at once, like taking the final step off the edge of a cliff. The dead came to him in his dream. They returned, as he knew they would, to haunt him with their curses and pleading. But this time he was among them.

Now he had joined their ranks lined up for dress parade. He stood among them in a ripped and bloodied uniform, his body strangely numb, though filled with grapeshot. His chest was an open wound framed by woolen blue. Looking down he saw the gaping jagged hole and at its center a stubborn heart, big as a grown man's fist, beating like a frightened rabbit's. The torn flesh did not bleed. It was the wound of a dead man. Great white maggots, hundreds of them, crawled blindly over his pale flesh, edging their way to the pumping heart. Yet his heart still beat. It pumped so hard he thought it would burst, explode. A pair of filthy hands Shiloh recognized as his own rose to the wound to quiet the pounding in his ruined chest, as he would a small bird.

In his dream Shiloh could feel his mouth contort with the horror of it. Yet no scream issued from a throat tightened with panic and fear.

And then there were bells—a thousand ringing bells—not church bells, nor the bells of steam engines, more like a school marm's bell, rung angrily at a tardy class.

Shiloh awoke in a spasm of startled panic. First he thought he was drowning, then he could feel the cold water soaking through his bedroll and clothes. Blinking his eyes open he saw the boy standing at the bars with a bucket in one hand and the pistol in the other. Beside him was the sheriff, looking grim and holding a handful of paper.

Daylight shone through the barred window of the cell and through the door to the sheriff's office.

''Mornin',' ' the sheriff called tentatively as Shiloh pulled himself from the soaking bunk. ''Amos here saw you were having a little trouble and called for me. You feelin' out of sorts, friend?''

Shivering, Shiloh rubbed the sleep from his eyes. ''Bad dream is all.''

As he stepped closer the sheriff shuffled through the yellow telegraph slips. ''Being locked up will do it to a man,'' he said. ''I got a fistful of replies back from my telegraphs last night. Care to hear what they say?''

Pulling his boots on, Shiloh considered the sheriff and boy who stood before him, on the other side of the bars. ''Don't that boy ever talk?''

The lawman looked from Shiloh to the boy, Amos, and then back again. ''No, as a matter of fact, he don't. He ain't deaf, he can hear better'n you or me, but he don't talk. Never has and I expect never will.''

"How'd he fetch you back?" Shiloh asked, walking to the bars.

"Show him, Amos," the sheriff instructed the boy.

With only a small bashful glance to Shiloh, the boy walked to the desk and picked up a battered cowbell and rang it, timidly at first, and then harder.

"That's enough, Amos," the sheriff said, smiling back over his shoulder. "Now 'bout these replies. I seem to have a mighty odd bird locked in my jail, and I just ain't sure what to do 'bout him."

"A cup of coffee and breakfast would be a good start," Shiloh offered.

Again the sheriff turned to face the boy who now sat on a chair by the desk, gun across his lap. "Amos, go fetch some breakfast for Mr. Shiloh here and bring some coffee."

The boy was out the door as soon as the sheriff finished talking.

"Now, 'bout these responses," the lawman said, turning to Shiloh. "Here's an interesting one: 'To the best of our knowledge, Henry Proffitt, known as Shiloh, has operated within the law in regard to all of his dealings with this company. The Wells, Fargo & Company will not accept responsibility for this individual or for any acts which he is suspected of committing. L. F. Rowell, Assistant Supervisor of Wells, Fargo & Company.' "

Shiloh made no reply.

"Now that ain't exactly a love letter, is it?" the sheriff said. "But they spent a pretty penny sending it, that was a 'repeated message' too."

The thought of a Fargo man sitting behind a desk trying

to figure out how to save the company's reputation made Shiloh smile. "They said I wasn't a wanted man."

"No, and in their own way I suppose they said that at least the company knew who you were. Here's another one, this one from the federal marshal. 'Shiloh not a criminal at last report. Do not advance government money without approval of this office.' "

Again, this brought a smile to Shiloh's face.

The sheriff's smile faded. He was not a man who was happy at being double-talked to by the likes of Wells, Fargo & Company nor the federal marshal's office. "Well, I'm just happy as a fat hog in sunshine that you are enjoyin' yerself. Care to hear what the Pinkerton Agency had to say?"

"More of the same I suppose," Shiloh answered.

"Yes, more of the same indeed. Except the one from this town up north, Splendid. The sheriff up there was a mite stingy with words. He just said, 'Shoot the sonofabitch.' Lord knows how he got it past the telegraph operator. I take it you don't have many friends up that part of the country?"

Shiloh considered the lawman, who was now building to a proper rage. "No, not many."

"Mr. Shiloh, you care to tell me what you exactly are?"

"Yes, sir," Shiloh replied. "I guess you would call me a bounty hunter."

The sheriff studied Shiloh for a moment, then walked quietly back to his desk. Placing the telegraph messages neatly down, the lawman picked up a deck of cards that sat in one corner. He turned over the first card, examined it, and buried it back in the deck. Then he began cutting the deck, one-handed, working the cards smoothly along his palm while he thought of what to say next. "Well, that's just real nice. Just the kind of visitor we like in town,'' he said as he worked the cards faster. ''Hell, you might even wanta come around to the church social we got planned. Maybe give a speech at the school.''

And then Amos came through the door with Shiloh's breakfast.

12

At dusk, Sheriff B. Z. Walker opened the cage that held Shiloh. He pulled the keys off the wall slowly and opened the door with hesitation. Then, while Shiloh waited by the lawman's desk for his guns, the sheriff came to a complete stop.

Standing behind his desk, hands on his hips and his hat pushed back, the sheriff looked Shiloh over. "I don't have to give you these, you know that."

"I know that, Sheriff," Shiloh said, meeting the lawman's steady gaze. "But you seem a fair man. And I know you will."

"Now, that's a bet I'd copper," the lawman mumbled even as he dug Shiloh's rig from his desk drawer. "You care to hear what the other telegraphs said? Last one came in 'bout an hour ago."

Taking his gunbelt from the sheriff, Shiloh strapped it on. "I reckon they weren't too different from the first batch."

"No, 'bout the same. The federal marshal up near Bodie sent two. The first said that he never hearda you breakin' the law. The second was to tell you that there weren't any more criminals up there, so you shouldn't bother yerself with ridin' his way. Seems all Bodie's criminals have gone to Texas.''

Drawing the Colt from its holster, Shiloh clicked out the cylinder and inspected the cartridges. Noticing two spent shells, he plucked them out, replaced them with two from his belt, and clicked the cylinder closed. ''Well, that was plenty thoughtful, wasn't it?''

''I ain't so certain he was worried 'bout your business affairs, so much as his own,'' the sheriff answered, handing over Shiloh's Winchester from a rack behind his desk. ''If it's all the same, I would prefer keeping those Springfields.''

The sheriff watched somberly as Shiloh checked the action of the rifle, pumped a shell into the chamber, emptied the magazine, checked the gun's action, then reloaded.

''If yer don't mind my askin', Shiloh ain't yer given name, is it? Those other fellas they called you Proffitt, didn't they?''

''No, it ain't given, I suppose I just sorta up and took it,'' Shiloh said, returning to the cell to retrieve his bedroll. The saddle lay on the floor in front of the sheriff's desk. Retying the roll to the saddle, he pulled out the blue woolen Union coat for warmth against the night chill.

''Shiloh. It seems to me that I heard that before, Bible readin'. Am I right?''

''You're a good man, B. Z. Walker, 'bout the best sheriff I run across in a while,'' Shiloh said, pulling on the wool coat and then turning again to the lawman. ''It's a fine thing for a lawman to be up on his Bible.'' When Shiloh stood again, he was hefting the saddle in one hand, up over his shoulder, and held the Winchester repeater in the other. "But I didn't borrow the name from the good book."

And then the sheriff saw. It came to him in an instant, the dusty stranger standing in front of his desk, wearing the stripped-down Union coat, the holster with the stamped "U.S." still visible, even though it had been cut away and mended into quick-draw fashion. "Good Lord, you were there," he whispered. "You couldn'ta been old enough. You ain't old enough."

"There a hotel in town?" Shiloh asked, feeling the weight of the saddle and the lawman's questions bear down on him. Suddenly the room had become very small, smaller even than the cell in which he had spent the night.

The sheriff continued to stare, measuring the man who stood before him. Behind the widened eyes, his brain calculated Shiloh's age, studied the bits of shabby uniform, patched and repatched. And finally he knew it to be true.

"Sheriff, about that hotel?" Shiloh asked, turning slightly toward the door. It was the first time he had seen the sheriff startled.

"The hotel is down the street aways, halfway through town," came the response. "It ain't fancy, but it's clean. More like a rooming house than a hotel. Run by a maiden lady."

"Thank you, Sheriff, I'm obliged to you," Shiloh said, and stepped out the door into the town's evening bustle of activity.

They rode in at last light. Burrows and Follard came down the hills and into town from the east. They rode stirrup to stirrup, talking casually as they passed through the center of town. Marcus Stemper rode in by himself, almost in darkness from the west. And Randy Stemper followed, on foot, leaking out from between the cafe and general merchandise store onto the darkened street. Pausing, he surveyed the town, stepped up on the boards, and strolled to the nearest saloon.

B. Z. Walker was in his office playing solitaire. He dealt the cards expertly, with a precise snap of the wrist and without missing a single play. But he took no pleasure in the game. Instead, he was wondering what kind of man he had let free in his town. The boy came into the office so quietly that it was a long time before the sheriff looked up.

"What is it, Amos?" the sheriff asked, putting the cards down in front of him. "You see something?"

The boy nodded yes, his head working up and down rapidly.

"There a fight, someone fighting?"

The boy shook his head and raised four fingers.

"Strangers in town. Four of them?"

The boy nodded.

Coming up from behind his desk, the sheriff reached out and held the boy's shoulder. It was a fatherly gesture, though the sheriff was not his father. "When did they come in, all four, just now?"

The boy shook his head, held up two fingers.

"Two together, good. And the others?"

The boy held up one finger.

"Then one, and the other?"

The boy made a motion, like a man walking with two fingers.

"Good boy, three riding and one walking. You think that they're the men that Shiloh was talking about?"

The boy shrugged, not knowing what to signal.

"They look like miners, cowpokes, or what?"

Again Amos shrugged, then thought better of it, and shook his head.

"That's fine, real fine, now you go down to the cafe and get supper, I'll be along shortly, then we'll go play some cards over at the Son."

The boy was halfway out the door when the lawman called to him. "Amos, you got your bell?"

Stopping, the boy turned hesitantly from the door and returned into the office to retrieve the bell from the slat-backed chair where it rested. Then, going over to the sheriff's desk, he picked up a sheet of paper and stuffed it into the bell.

The sheriff watched the procedure, well aware that the boy was shy about carrying the clanging bell around. But the bell would have to do until the next best thing came along. "That's fine now. Amos, you get along."

And with that the boy jammed the bell into the pocket of his casekeeper coat and walked quickly out through the doorway and into the darkness.

Sam Follard and Clayton Burrows were resting their elbows over the polished wood of the Happy Gal Saloon. Two glasses filled with liquor waited in front of them and three tables of poker progressed behind their backs. Follard, as was his habit, stood at the bar in a comfortable half turn, talking to his companion and watching the door at the same time.

"Now, then, my loyal friend, I say we toast you with the first drink," Follard said, beaming his best drummer smile at Clayton, who stood facing him with a half-opened mouth.

"Me? But I didn't do nothin'?" the big man answered, more than a little surprised.

"Nothing? My dear friend and factotum? Nothing? But we drink not to what you did, but what you are about to do!" Follard bellowed, his voice loud enough to turn the bar-dog's attention away from a group of miners at the end of the bar. It was as much the noise as Follard's appearance. For by any standards, it was an odd sight to see the ill-dressed stranger, thick with the dust of the trail, unshaven, and certainly not bathed, begin spouting ten-dollar words at a two-bit saloon, even if he was wearing a brocade vest.

"Oh, I forgot," Clayton said slowly as Follard urged his hand with the drink up to the big man's thick, cracked lips. "What was it I was to do, agin?"

"Why, my dear Clayton, you jest, you are too, too modest, but remember, humbleness is not a virtue. No, my dear friend, not a virtue in the least," Follard said loudly as he turned briefly to signal the bartender for another drink.

"No, Sam, I forgot, I did," Clayton lamented, now genuinely worried that he had forgotten something of great consequence.

The barkeep, who had hurried down from the end of the bar, refilled the two glasses and collected the coins promptly. "If you gents don't mind my askin', is one of you a preacher? We, the boys an' me, couldn't help but hear you going on, preaching like."

"Preacher, why damned no and no again! Though in fact you honor me with such a title," Follard answered. "We, my companion and I, are just two travelers on life's highway, looking for what fortune may await us."

"Don't worry, boys, he ain't here to save ya miserable souls, sell ya some patent medicine more likely!" the bardog called back to the small group of men at the far end of the bar. The news was greeted with a mild ripple of laughter.

"Thanks, gents, just wanted to clear that up," the aproned bartender said, turning again to Follard and Clayton. "Jest don't sell 'im anything that'll get 'im drunker than my liquor."

"It true you got a gal in this town that went wit the King a Spain?" Clayton asked, no longer able to hold his curiosity. "I heard it from a saloon keeper in Creed."

"I s'pose that's as true as anything else you be likely to hear in Creed. An' if the King of Spain had a notion and five dollars, well, then, it's a genuine possibility."

The bartender was already halfway down the bar when Clayton called after him. "I heard she was a Frenchie gal! Real purty, with red hair!"

"Listen to me, Clay, now pay attention and quit worryin' 'bout the King of Spain," Follard said, his hand out on Burrows's thick arm, fingers digging into the knotted muscles. "You remember what you must do, a little job we talked about?"

"No, Sam, honest I forgot it," Burrows said pleadingly.

Follard took his hand off the big man's arm, then reached down and handed him up his fresh drink. "Now, listen and don'tcha forget it again, 'cause it is important," Follard coaxed.

Taking a small sip, Burrows looked down at Follard with as serious an expression as he could manage. "I ain't gonna forget it agin, tell me, Sam."

"Now listen, when we find the fellow who's been following us, you kill him. You shoot that sonofabitch dead!"

13

Shiloh found the hotel easily. Just as Sheriff Walker told him.

A thin, tired-looking woman in faded calico welcomed him at the door. She studied Shiloh for a long time in a long, assessing stare that sized him up from boots to hat before speaking. Shiloh studied her right back. She rested one hand on her hip, the other on the handle of a worn broom. So bony thin and small-looking was she, Shiloh imagined that she could put her full weight on the broom and not so much as bend one of the dried bristles at its end. "The price is three dollars a night," she said, sweeping a stray length of graying hair back onto her head. "That will get you your own bed and two meals a day. You can take them either in your room or with the rest of the guests."

"That's fine," Shiloh answered, stepping through the door. But the woman did not follow him. Waiting at the door, she looked over her new guest carefully before speaking. "In advance."

It was only after first examining and then pocketing the coins that she led Shiloh through a small parlor, a larger dining room, and up a set of stairs. As they walked, she recited the house rules. "We don't allow lady callers, swearing, or any nonsense with guns."

"That's fine," Shiloh answered as he followed her up the narrow stairway.

"There is, I believe, an establishment in town that caters to those particular vices. I'm certain that someone at the barbershop or livery will be pleased to give you directions, if your interests lie in that form of activity."

"Thank you, ma'am."

"I will not tolerate gambling in this house, and when you take your meals with the other guests, I expect you to be fully clothed, undergarments will not do, not at all."

"I'll see to it, ma'am."

"The water in the rooms is changed daily; the conveniences are in the back. Please try not to frighten the chickens at night if you find it necessary to use the facilities."

"I'll try, ma'am."

"Here we are," she said, coming to a door at the end of the hall and turning toward Shiloh. "I hope this suits your tastes, Mr. . . ."

"Shiloh."

"Mr. Shiloh. Have a pleasant evening."

"Thank you, ma'am."

As she walked back down the hall, Shiloh couldn't help but notice that she may have been thin as a stick, but in this house she was as much the law as the sheriff, B. Z. Walker.

Lighting the kerosene lamp, Shiloh looked over the room. It was as neat and clean as the downstairs of the house. The bed looked comfortable enough. There was a quilt laid across it for cold nights, and the curtains, though old and faded, were clean. Shiloh had slept in worse places and paid more.

Three buildings down and across a narrow alley, the Stempers were bedding down in the livery. Although they each had nearly five hundred dollars in their saddlebags and pockets, they preferred the livery. The few times they had rented rooms had proven disastrous, with either one or the both of them breaking some unstated rule and having to face the wrath of a landlord or the humiliating stares of some tinhorn drummer.

A loft with fresh hay above a livery was cheaper, and suited their needs just right.

"Know what I was jest thinkin', Marcus?" the younger brother, Randy, asked, reclining against a sack of oats.

"How in hell would I know'd what you was thinkin'?" came the answer from Marcus, who was busy fiddling with the wick of a dented lantern.

"I was jest thinkin' how come it is Follard gets an equal share? He didn't do nothin' back there at the Fargo coach."

Striking a lucifer against a beam over his head, Marcus lifted the chimney from the lamp and lit it. A yellow kerosene glow bathed the loft. "Nothin' but lead us on the proper trail, know'd when the stage was comin', and . . ."

"Shee-it and green apples, me or ya coulda done that."

"Then why didn't we?" Marcus asked as he scratched his beard. Though he was barely out of his twenties, the thick beard was already streaked with gray. He knew, too well, where his brother was leading, but not so sure he wanted to follow. Randy was a strange one, even Marcus would admit that. Their momma said it was " 'cause he got the fever" when he was just a baby.

"We didn't 'cause we didn't thinka it," Randy replied, pulling his gun from its cross-draw holster. "But I know'd you ain't sayin' we couldn'ta."

"What kinda thing is that? What in hell is that s'pose to mean?"

"I ain't gonna dress it up for ya in some twenty-dollar suit and boiled shirt to trot 'er out," Randy said, studying the cartridges in the open chamber of his gun. "It means, pure and simple as pie, if Sam Follard was to die like, we, botha us, could take his money. Hell, I was half thinkin'a doin' it back there when we took the stage, but that sumbitch got started shootin'."

Marcus watched his brother carefully in the uneven light. The loft grew very quiet, even the street below them seemed to grow quiet. The only sound was that of Randy, rolling the cylinder of the pistol, first one way, then the other. At each turn it would click twice, pause, then click two more times.

"First it was Malley," Marcus said at last. He spoke slowly and softly, like he was talking to a judge. "Now you wanta shoot Follard."

Randy clicked closed the cylinder and spun it again, like a casino wheel. "Malley was a low-down cheat, ya know'd it. Ya seen 'im that night, cheatin' at cards. No man cheats me at cards!"

"Malley was a greenhorn kid," Marcus answered patiently. "He could no more cheat than a hog cain fly. I backed yer play 'cause yer my brother, and he weren't nothin' to me. But that kid, he weren't cheatin'."

"He was a cheatin' bastard an' got what was comin' to 'im!"

Marcus studied his little brother carefully, trying to see if Randy really in truth believed what he was saying. Then he remembered the time when Randy was barely big enough to walk. He got ahold of an old mouser they had and cut its head off with their momma's best kitchen knife.

Remembering that, Marcus knew that it didn't matter a fiddler's damn what Randy believed about Malley.

"When I cut his throat, it was smooth as butter on a hot day," Randy said, drawing his knife out from its boot sheath. "Barely had to press and that soft skin just parted like silk. He was purely surprised." As he spoke, Randy Stemper drew the knife slowly in the air, showing his brother how easy it had been.

Watching, Marcus felt his throat go dry. "And ya did a fine joba that, too. He weren't but nicked. Coulda cut hisself worse shaving if he had anythin' to shave."

"Indians say that if ya look inta the eyes a the man ya kill in battle, ya get his strength. His strength kinda leaks inta yer, through his dyin' eyes."

"Shee-it, in battle," Marcus said disgustedly as he unwrapped his bedroll. "Ya hit that boy with a rock, and 'fore he hadda chance to git hisself up, ya were on 'im with that damned knife."

Randy stopped his imaginary throat-slicing and began to study the blade of the knife in the dull light of the lamp. Satisfied with what he saw, he slipped it back into his boot sheath. "Ah, well, I don't believe that Indian stuff no way."

"That boy could fight, though, even with a slit throat and bleeding like all get out, he was a fighter," Marcus said. "He was a kid with gumption and spunk for two."

But Randy wasn't listening anymore. Sliding the knife back into its sheath, he stretched out on the fresh hay, saddle under his head, and closed his eyes. In a few minutes he was asleep, snoring loudly as the kerosene lamp with its cracked chimney cast its yellowish, uneven light over his sharp-featured face.

Marcus watched his brother sleep. There was a time, he could even now remember, that they had been like real brothers. But that was so long ago. Now in his memory they both seemed like two different people. They had been riding for five years. A long time by Marcus's reckoning. And, he had to offer, it wasn't all bad. They had their share of good times. Spending money from pockets heavy with coin. Those were the times that Marcus liked to remember. Those fancy saloons, with the short-skirted waiter gals and bottles of liquor with foreign names so strange that you just pointed, never knowing if it was going to be sweet or burn like the devil's own piss.

And then there was the gambling. They had themselves a fine time out in Colorado, bucking the tiger at faro. The money went faster then. It went faster across those damned tables than drinking it up or pressing it into the hands of some pretty box rustler. Oh, lordy, Marcus thought to himself, they lost a damn fortune betting badger fights. And then more, betting against a bull terrier in a fight against a bobcat. Oh, lordy, who coulda guessed. But they had themselves a time.

Then it all started to turn bad. Randy started the killing, like someone was betting against him.

Marcus reached into his vest pocket and brought out a package of Durham and papers. Watching Randy sleep, he rolled himself a smoke and lit it off the flame from the lamp.

No, Marcus thought to himself, Randy never was quite right. "Tetched in the haid," is what Poppa had said. First it was little things, like mice and barn bats, and such. And then the cat, but nobody knew. And then that teacher lady, new in town and full of do-gooding notions, tried to teach Randy spelling and reading. Fifteen and big as a grown man, but he couldn't read a damned feed sack let alone the gospel. And she tried to teach him.

It was Marcus who found her out by the smokehouse,

her horse and buggy tied right next to the body. The summer Kansas sun just hot as hell. Marcus was soaked through with sweat by the time he ran and got Randy. He was sitting by the creek in the dry grass with his shirt off, smiling as he washed the blood off his arms.

Marcus could remember saddling the horses and taking the food. They rode for three days, never mentioning the teacher lady. And now five years of riding and robbing were behind them. Just as quick as going to sleep and waking up in the morning.

Clearing a small spot on the floor, Marcus stubbed out the smoke with his boot toe. Then he took his boots off and stretched out on the worn bedroll. Before turning down the lamp, he took a final look over at Randy, who had curled into a small ball on the floor. Somewhere out on the trail it had all changed. The money spent quicker, the gals weren't ever quite pretty enough, and the whiskey all tasted the same. Everything had just turned bad. Now that they were with Follard, Marcus hoped their luck would change, but somehow he doubted it.

14

AMOS SAW THEM leave the saloon after midnight. The big one was weaving, holding his hat in one hand and leaning against the little one with the other. As Amos watched from the shadows of an alley, Burrows and Follard made their way down the center of the empty street toward the whorehouse.

"I doan give a good rat's ass whata King a Spain pays, I ain't never paid more'n ten dollars for it in me life, an' I ain't 'bout ta start neither," the big one said. "Kings an' such, they got them crowns an' such, bagsa rubies, dimans an such, whata they care. Toss some painted cat, diman big as a hen egg. They doan care."

"My dear and sociable friend," Follard began with a grand wave of his hand. "I want you to go up to that house and damn the price, no matter. You pick out the loveliest of the lovelies, and it will be I who pays. Up to twenty dollars, of course."

At that, Clayton stopped dead in his tracks and turned to face Follard on shaky legs. "Twenty dollars, you doan think she cost that much?"

"For the Spanish king's own concubine and intimate, she may just," Follard replied, knowing full well Clayton had about as much chance of finding the King of Spain's mistress in a Nevada whorehouse as they had of finding the king himself emptying washbasins in the same establishment.

But Follard himself was not totally disbelieving that the Spanish king's favorite was a fallen woman. In his own imagination he pictured the dark-eyed lovely draped in lace and silks, reclining provocatively across a divan while she awaited her Morgan or Vanderbilt callers. She would be in New York, of course. In a richly paneled room lit by the gentle and civilized glow of gas.

Indeed, that is where Follard himself imagined he belonged, and not the consort of bumpkins and half-wits. His rightful place was in New York, riding in fine carriages, waited on by obsequious uniformed servants, and carrying on intrigues with the pampered ladies of the very best society one night, and matching wits with their husbands over fine port and cigars the next. That Follard knew to be his rightful place. And after he had made his fortune in this godforsaken wilderness, he would claim his proper place.

"Whoa, no I can't ask you . . ." Clayton said as he started to walk again. "Nothin's worth . . ."

"But you are, my friend, you are. Just remember your job and what you have to do about our desert friend."

"Oh, I ain't forgettin' now, no, sir, Sam," Clayton vowed.

"Good then, and I fully intend to pay."

"Sam, wanna hear somethin'?" Clayton began and continued before Follard could answer. "I hear this down in Yuma, an' it works. You wanna get the most from a whore, you hurt 'er. Not like a lot, but a little bitty, like pinch 'er. It works good, too.''

''I shall keep that in mind in all my romantic encounters, thank you, Clayton,'' Follard replied as they strolled down the street.

When the two men passed, Amos ran directly to the sheriff. Sheriff Walker was already up on one elbow, squinting at the doorway when Amos charged into the small room that served as the law's sleeping quarters.

''That you, Amos?'' the sheriff asked and, hearing no response, knew that it was. ''What is it, boy? You see something?''

Taking a match from the tin by the door, Amos struck it and lit the lantern.

''What is it? Fight?''

Amos shook his head and held up four fingers.

''The strangers, is that Shiloh jasper with 'em?''

Again Amos shook his head.

''They doin' something?''

Amos held up two fingers on each hand.

Squinting in the harsh glow of the light, the sheriff twisted his face into a knot. ''They two an' two.''

Amos nodded.

''What are they doin'?''

Amos, putting his hands together and lying his head against them, made like he was sleeping.

''They sleeping? That ain't against the law,'' the sheriff said, easing himself back down into the blanket.

Amos shook his head and held up two fingers.

''Two of 'em sleeping. What the other two doin'?''

This presented a serious problem for the boy. The last time he signaled trouble in the town's most famous house, the sheriff had boxed his ears, but good. First he looked toward the wall, then let his eyes slip to the floor, where he stared at a space between the worn toes of his boots.

"Hell, Amos, that ain't against the law neither!" the sheriff said, smiling his annoyance.

Amos continued to stare at the floor, figuring that he had done wrong to wake the sheriff.

"Amos, you done fine, boy," Walker consoled. "Least we knows where they are an' that they ain't goin' nowheres tonight. Now, you git along to sleep."

By the time Amos turned down the wick and blew out the lantern's dim flame, the sheriff was already halfways asleep. Walking silently out of the room and through the office, the boy made his way casually along the boards.

If the truth were known, he was no stranger to Silver Creek's house of ill repute. Barely fifteen, he had been going there for as long as he could remember. Not that he actually went upstairs with any of the girls, rather, he went to smell the sweet orchid and lilac scent of the perfume and to have the girls fuss over him, feeding him cakes and mussing his hair as he sat on the back porch.

Amos liked Silver Creek's saloons as well, the music from the piano and the lies the men told as the hour grew late.

Leaving the sheriff's office, he vanished into the darkness of a narrow alley and half ran around the back to the house. As he entered the small yard, the boy heard someone call his name.

"Amos, that you?"

Stepping out from the shadows and into the light from the back window, he saw Emily. Barely older than he was, Emily was his favorite girl in the house, maybe his favorite girl in the whole town. She was sitting on the porch, barefoot, with her blue dress unbuttoned just enough to reveal her gray-faded underthings.

"Don't be creeping around in the dark. Come sit with a girl and be some company," Emily teased.

Eagerly Amos complied, hurrying over to the slanted steps where she sat. He was rewarded by a playful tousle of his hair.

"Don't have no cookies if that's what you comin' 'round for," she said.

Amos shrugged slightly to show that the cookies weren't important, though not the furthest thing from his mind either.

"Well then, what you doin' walking 'round this late, likely to scare decent folks halfta death?"

Again, Amos shrugged. But now he was serious, his face turned mournfully toward the girl's.

"What's wrong, Amos?" she asked, arranging herself slightly to get a better look at the boy in the dim light.

Amos began to shrug again, then changed his mind and held up two fingers.

"Two what? Two hours, two days, two dollars?"

Amos shook his head and pledged to himself that if ever the good Lord gave him a voice, Emily would be the first person he would talk to. He would ask her to leave with him, first thing.

Standing, Amos stuck his thumbs into his belt, puffed out his chest, and again held up two fingers.

"Two men?"

He nodded.

"Two men here?"

Amos nodded again and pointed to Emily.

"Two men to see me, two gentlemen callers."

Shrugging, Amos lifted his hand high above his head and then lowered it so that it was level with his eyes.

"Two men, big and small, here to see me."

Then, in a burst of frustration, Amos grabbed Emily by

the shoulders and shook her, and shook his head. He had never touched her like that before and the sudden movement startled the girl. "Amos!" she cried. "Amos! Let go! Let go!"

But he couldn't. He just kept shaking her. He shook her so hard that her hair, piled high on her head and held with pins, came loose and tumbled down over her eyes and shoulders. He had to make her understand. He had to make her understand that he was watching these men for the sheriff. And he wanted, desperately, to tell her that he believed that fella Shiloh's story, even if the sheriff didn't.

Finally, in a surprising fit of strength, she pulled his hands from her shoulders. "Amos! Stop! This instant!" she cried.

Though he had already stopped and was standing in front of her, shaking with frustration and fear.

And then they heard it. The sound of breaking glass from inside the house. It froze both of them, as still as a tintype in the dull light of the back porch.

Then there was more breaking glass and a woman's scream. When she heard the scream, Emily bounded to her feet and made for the door. Amos tried to grab for her, but the wisp of skirt he managed to touch slid over the tops of his fingers and she was through the back door.

He heard the scream again as a top window over his head exploded outward, and glass showered around his head as a water pitcher shattered at his feet.

Without thinking, Amos dragged the bell from his pocket and began waving it furiously. But the bell made no sound. In a panic, he realized the bell was mute as he was and pumped his arm furiously. Then he remembered the paper that held the clapper.

Tearing the paper out from the bell, he began ringing it

again, this time as he ran skidding around the alley and out into the street toward the sheriff's office.

B. Z. Walker was on the boards, naked from the waist up, buckling on his holster with one hand and holding a shotgun in the other.

"Amos! What is it, boy? What's the commotion?"

Amos skidded to a stop, turned, and ran in the other direction, still ringing the bell with the sheriff following.

As they entered the backyard to the whorehouse, they heard the shot. Amos was halfway up the stairs when he felt the sheriff's large hand clamp down on his shoulder and pull him off. "You stay here, son," Walker said, cocking the shotgun, his eyes fastened on the back door. "This ain't no place for you."

Amos fell backward off the two steps of the porch and watched the sheriff stride through the door. When the sheriff's form was no longer visible from the bottom of the porch steps, Amos followed.

Inside it smelled like lilacs, whiskey, and cigars. Instinctively Amos inhaled deeply, nearly forgetting why he was there.

Then there was more glass breaking upstairs and the sound of running feet. Four or five people running across the loose boards of the upper floor. They were running so hard, dust drifted down from the ceiling in the bright lamp light and settled on the blue velvet of the greeting couch.

The boy watched as the sheriff took the narrow stairs two at a time. More shouting followed. Amos could hear cussing then, men and women using the same words. Tears welled up in the boy's eyes. The two people he cared about most in town were up there with men who he knew were killers.

Desperately, he looked for a weapon and found the cane. An ash walking stick with an ivory handle leaned against one corner of the room. Grabbing the cane, he ran up the stairs, the length of hardened wood held high above his head with two hands.

When he reached the top of the stairs, he saw them. The two killers, stripped down to their underwear with the sheriff holding the shotgun on them. The girls stood around in a loose circle, Emily too, studying the men.

"I'll be damned if'n I knowed what happened, Sheriff," the owner, Mabe, said. "He jest went off, crazy like, commenced ta smashing my place to hell."

"Why, Sheriff, you bring a posse with you?" one of the girls, the one called Eve, chirped suddenly.

And then all eyes were on Amos, standing at the top of the darkened stairs, holding the cane.

It was the girls who laughed first, even Emily. Amos would always remember that. Even Emily had laughed at him. He stood there frozen, eyes growing wide, with his throat closing in so he couldn't breathe. Tears burned their way out again. He couldn't even bring the damned cane down from over his head.

Amos felt his face burning and knew it was turning bright red. Then the sheriff smiled and startled to chuckle, and so did the killers, even with a shotgun pointed at them.

Finally, he threw the cane down and ran. He ran down the stairs and out into the street, taking in deep lungfuls of the cool night air as the tears streamed down his face.

15

As far as B. Z. Walker could see, it was a simple matter. That is, simple after you stopped listening to the big one flapping his jaws about the King of Spain and a five-dollar whore and to the little one using ten-dollar words like they were a nickel a dozen. After a person stopped thinking about those things, then there was only a matter of an unpaid whore, a broken pitcher, and a busted window. Everything else, as far as the sheriff was concerned, you could throw to the hogs, ten-dollar words and all.

Soon they were all out on the back porch, the sheriff, Mabe, Burrows, and Follard. The sheriff held the shotgun on the two men, while Mabe stood off to the side, hands on her hips, like a stern school marm. "What you figurin' on doing, B. Z.?" Mabe asked finally, eyeballing the two men, Burrows and Follard, and not liking at all what she saw.

"You figure ten dollars will cover the damage?" the sheriff asked back without letting his gaze drop from the two men.

"That's 'bout right, seein' as that pitcher was a present

from a gentleman admirer of my early years. Ten dollars would be all right, I s'pose."

"You boys have ten dollars between ya?" the sheriff asked Burrows and Follard with a slight back and forth motion of the shotgun. They were both dressed, more or less, Burrows wearing his pants and shirt, and holding his boots in one hand. Follard, bare-chested, with one boot on and the other off.

Burrows turned to Follard to answer. "Why, Sheriff, as I explained earlier, we are perfectly amicable and able to pay for any damages incurred in this little misunderstanding."

"Then pay the lady, and we all can be on about our business," the sheriff shot back.

"Very well, Sheriff, I will be reaching into my trouser pocket to retrieve the money," Follard said, moving a hand cautiously toward his waist.

"I doan think yer should pay," Burrows cut in suddenly. "I can reckon the King a Spain never been here. An' that fat un," he said, angrily pointing to Mabe, "she lied, dirty down and all to us."

"Clayton, please, now is not the time to discuss it, we should put our differences aside as we reach this mutual understanding and financial compromise."

"I doan care!" Clayton insisted. "I axed 'er fair and simple 'bout the king, and she lied. She said, 'He was in every Saturday night.' Said ya could set yer watch by 'im. An' that ain't right, nohow."

"Clayton, let us pay this good woman and be on our way," Follard offered, bringing out a ten-dollar gold piece. "The longer we dally the worse it will get for all involved, isn't that right, Sheriff."

"That's about it," Walker replied, taking the coin and quickly handing it over to Mabe.

"Now, be a good lad, Clayton, and go back in and fetch my hat. I believe I left it in the parlor."

In an instant Clayton was back through the doors, leaving Follard, Mabe, and the sheriff standing in a loose circle around the porch.

"That boy ain't right, noway," Mabe said as the door slammed behind Clayton. "He's funny in the head?"

"Alas, yes," Follard replied. "A touch slow, but as big a heart as one could hope to find. And loyal, he is loyal to the death."

"You keep a close eye on him in town," Walker said, lowering the shotgun a notch. "I hear a word 'bout him on the street or in a saloon, he'll be spending the night in the lockup."

"Of course, Sheriff. I would not want to strain the hospitality of your good town. I assure you we will be on about our business as soon as possible."

The sheriff looked over the smooth talker carefully. He was dressed like a saddle tramp, except for the fancy vest he held rolled up in his arms, but spoke like some preacher or teacher. Whatever he was, the sheriff didn't like it. "And what 'xactly is your business?"

"A little of this and a little of that, we are at the mercy of the fates," Follard replied. "I myself am a trained and expert mixologist, having worked in drinking establishments from New Orleans to New York to Chicago. And my companion, he assists me in disposing of, let us say, undesirable clientele."

"Prob'ly deal a little faro, now and again. Maybe a little monte?"

"I have been known to participate in games of chance and skill."

"Poker too, I would say," the sheriff pressed.

"A gracious game, combining intellect and intestinal fortitude."

"We ain't got no call for bar-dogs, far as I know, and the games in town are all square. You keep that in mind. What about your friends?"

"Why, Sheriff, what friends? It is only poor Clayton and myself."

"Coupla boys up in the livery. They ain't with you?"

"Why, no, Sheriff, as I have stated, there is only Clayton and myself, traveling together on life's trail, doing the best for ourselves that we can."

With the reappearance of Burrows, the conversation died. He was standing in the lighted doorway, holding Follard's hat. "You know what one a them gals called me?" he asked, his face purple with rage. "Now, that ain't right, neither!"

Anxiously Follard's eyes darted around for a topic. With the sheriff still holding the scattergun on them, he assumed that they were not yet free to go about their business. And with Clayton babbling on about some whore, they may just spend a night under this local constable's jail-house roof. Spotting a scrap of paper in the dirt, he bent slowly to pick it up.

"Look, some poor unfortunate has misplaced a telegraph message," Follard said, unfolding the wrinkled and torn message. " 'Pity the rascal who goes against Shiloh and any lawman who has him in town,' " Follard read. "And it appears to be from a federal marshal in Elkton."

"I believe that telegraph is my property," the sheriff said, hand out to take it. "You boys can be on your way."

After the two men had left, Mabe looked over at the sheriff. The shotgun rested casually in the crook of his arm. "I be damned if I knowed where that came from," she said, indicating the telegraph message.

"Amos stuffed it in his bell, to keep it from ringing. Boy's become downright prickly 'bout that bell."

"Can ya blame 'im," Mabe shot back, suddenly becoming a school marm again. "Walkin' 'round town ringin' like a damn heffer."

"Can't think a nothin' else," the sheriff replied as way of apology.

"An' he ain't hardly a boy no more, neither," Mabe continued. "Almost a man. 'Nother year or two he ain't gonna be comin' 'round here for no cookies, neither."

Suddenly the sheriff was very much aware of being stripped from the waist up. A cool night breeze sent a chill through him. "I don't know whatta do with the boy," he replied, turning to face Mabe.

"What you do is you cut 'im loose directly," Mabe scolded. "I ain't sayin' it gonna happen, but what if, and only if, some young kid drunk on liquor an' all blows you to kingdom come. Then that boy ain't got nothin'! Nothin' in this world but a patcha dirt to put flowers on Sundays."

"You think I don't know it? That I ain't thought on it," the sheriff answered as he started to walk away.

"You git that youngster a job, over at the livery or writing numbers for the Fargo company," Mabe called after the sheriff.

"I'll think on it, Mabe," he replied, walking toward the alley.

"B. Z. Walker, don't you slink yerself away from me, not when I'm talkin' to yer."

The sheriff stopped as quickly as a schoolboy who'd been caught in some mischief. Turning, he faced Mabe across the narrow space of the alley.

"It was a fine thing what you done," she said, her voice now gentler. "Takin' Amos in when his folks died an' all. But ya gotta cut 'im loose, for his own sake."

"I know it," the sheriff said. "I jest can't bring myself to."

"Well, you gonna halfta," Mabe said even more softly. "Now, ya come in here and drink some tea, and put ona shirt I got. How does it look, sheriff an' all, leaving my house without a shirt."

At the livery, Amos made himself a bed of hay in an empty stall and covered himself with an old horse blanket hung across the door. Although he had stopped crying, his eyes still burned, and his chest felt like someone had taken a dozen turns around it with a length of rope.

By tomorrow, he knew the whole town would have heard that he had made a fool of himself at Mabe's, and they'd laugh at him. They wouldn't laugh to his face, none of 'em would do that, but they'd laugh and snicker behind his back. And the women with their parasols and mail-bought dresses, they'd giggle about it in the general merchandise store, covering their mouths as they pretended to look at the goods set out on the counter.

The more he thought on it, the worse it became. Even Emily had laughed at him. And so had the sheriff.

In the next stall a horse snorted and shifted its weight in its sleep. And soon, Amos could feel the hot rush of tears again. He knew that it would serve them all right if he lit off. Just saddled up a horse and took to the hills. There was an old line shack up there, where the sheriff and him went hunting and fishing. He could stay up there.

And then he heard the noise. It was like a scratching, only slower, smoother, and familiar. He knew that sound. Lifting his head from the coarse material of the blanket, Amos listened. It was coming regular now, a slow, patient kind of scratching.

Turning his head, Amos looked up and saw the lantern

light leaking through the floorboards from above. It was the other two killers. They were right above him. Then he recognized the sound. It was the sound of someone pulling a blade across a stone, sharpening a knife.

"Randy, what in hell you doin'?" came the first voice from above.

"Nothin' but putting an edge on this, may need it," came the reply.

"Are you a savage, goddamn, up in the middle a the night, sharpening a goddamn knife? What is wrong with you?"

Then there was no answer, just the steady pull of the steel blade over the stone. If anything, it grew louder, more insistent.

"Randy? Ya listenin' to me?"

"I hear ya, but I ain't gonna stop. Cain't sleep."

"Maybe ya shoulda gone with Clayton an' Sam. That woulda been more to yer liking?" the other replied, rolling over and making the floorboards creak.

"That ain't the plan, like ya said, and 'sides, I got no use for that half-wit and that snake-tongued bastard."

Rising slowly from the hay bed, Amos stood to hear better. Then there was some mumbling he couldn't hear. Walking to the door, he stood in the shadows by the foot of the ladder, waiting for the two to speak again.

Now, Amos was sweating. The past humiliation forgotten. If he could help B.Z. catch the killers in some thieving, they would forget about what happened at Mabe's. Maybe B.Z. would deputize him, like he was always joking and saying he would.

16

SHILOH WOKE FROM the night's terrors into daylight. Pulling on his pants and boots, he rose from the bed and looked out onto Silver Creek's narrow, red-dirt street. It was fully day now, and Shiloh didn't doubt that he had slept through breakfast.

Wagons and horses paraded down its center, their drivers and riders tipping their hats in neighborly morning welcomes. The scattering of strollers on the boards across the street chatted in the bright morning sun.

And then the street changed. Something was happening on the main street of Silver Creek. Riders pulled up on their reins and turned in their saddles. A ranch wagon, filled with sacks of grain and nail kegs, halted, its driver rising from the plank seat to turn and stare.

Shiloh watched through the clear glass of the window as the Fargo man, looking uncomfortable on a horse, rode by, grim-faced and twitchy in the saddle. And then came the children, running anxious and noisy down the street, stealing looks backward at the strange spectacle that followed.

They were bringing the Fargo coach back into town. Pulled by six mules, the sheriff's deputies had rigged up a new wheel, larger than the others. It tilted the coach more than slightly to one side.

As the smashed side of the Concord rolled by his window, Shiloh could see the bodies inside. They were wrapped in the canvas as Shiloh had left them. Slits made by the search party in the gray material revealed the faces of the dead men, stretched out on the floor of the doorless coach.

An old-timer in a slouch hat sat up on the Concord's seat, urging his team on with a familiar hand and shooing the children away from the opened side.

Activity on the street stopped dead as the strange vehicle passed, led by the Fargo man in front and three tired-looking riders behind.

After washing the dirt from his eyes at the basin, he put on his hat and walked the narrow stairs into the parlor. Seeing the boardinghouse in the light of day did not surprise him. It was as spotless and ordered as Shiloh knew it would be, under the careful eye of the landlady. Walking through the empty rooms, he followed the noise of chickens to the back of the building. There, in the harsh mid-morning light, was the landlady, feeding five or six pecking and bickering chickens from a worn sack of grain.

Shiloh watched from the door as the landlady scooped a hand into the sack and scattered the grain. Each handful was carefully measured. She dipped her hand to the sack three times before Shiloh spoke up. "Morning, ma'am, appears I slept through breakfast."

"Breakfast and nearly supper," came the brisk reply. She answered without turning from her chores. Shiloh watched her from the door, scattering the feed with a sharp, no-nonsense swing of her arm. She looked older in daylight. He could see that now as her face, turned in half profile, revealed leathery skin and graying hair. She looked older, but stronger too. Shiloh could see it in the way she stood ramrod straight. And he could see it when she turned clear around to meet his gaze with two sky-blue eyes, as hard as pebbles.

"Sorry, ma'am," Shiloh said. "It was a long ride, and I guess I was just more tired out than I thought."

She kept staring at Shiloh with two unblinking eyes, even as she wiped her hands briskly across the aproned front of the worn brown dress. "Not me you got to apologize to. Apologize to your stomach. I reckon it'll be complaining soon enough."

She walked up the three stairs to the porch with such rigid determination that Shiloh moved from her way before she hit the second step. "Never had a hired killer in my house before. Never intended to," she said, passing Shiloh and entering the kitchen. "But the good Lord does have a plentiful supply of surprises. Doesn't he, Mr. Shiloh?"

"That he does, ma'am," Shiloh answered, following her into the kitchen. On the table, which was white from a light dusting of flour, sat three pans of bread set out to rise.

"May I inquire who said I was a hired killer?" Shiloh asked as he cast an eye toward the large pot of coffee that sat steaming on the cast-iron stove.

"You'd do better to ask who hasn't. That old fool Red, in the telegraph, has been havin' a reg'lar picnic spreading the news through town. I see you don't wear your guns when you wake. I was under the impression that men in your profession wore their guns to bed."

"But I'm not in bed, ma'am," Shiloh said, edging his way closer to the coffeepot. He could smell it now.

"So you're not," was all that she answered, though Shiloh thought he could see a touch of a smile turn the corners of the thin mouth upward, just a little.

"I sure would be obliged for a cup of that coffee," Shiloh said.

But before she could answer, the sheriff strode through the door, hat in hand. "Mornin', missus, sure would be obliged for a cup of that coffee." And with that he sat himself down at the table.

"Sheriff, I sure must apologize for not hearing the news," she answered, facing the lawman across the floured expanse of tabletop.

"What news you talkin' 'bout, Miss Rachel?"

"News that Ben over at the café snuck out of town in the middle of the night, packed up and left. Figure I should count my blessings, me with the only coffee in town."

But she was already pulling down two cups from the cupboard, giving each one a close inspection before she set them in front of Shiloh and the sheriff.

"Thank you, ma'am," both men mumbled as she sat the cups down in front of them, then moved back to the stove to fetch the pot. "It's hot 'nough for the likes of you and so thick you can stand a spoon up in it. S'pose that's the way you like it."

"Thank you, Miss Rachel, I'm obliged," the sheriff said, lifting the cup to his lips. "Reason I'm 'round is that I'm lookin' for Amos. Ain't seen 'im since last night."

Shiloh took a sip from the thick cup and knew that she wasn't lying about it. It was strong and hot, in fact, just the way Shiloh did like it.

"What kind of trouble that boy in now?" she answered, carefully arranging the covered loaves of bread on the counter. Shiloh could tell her question was more than curiosity; the woman's entire back seemed to tense with the sheriff's mention of the boy.

"Had some trouble last night, and the boy took off," the sheriff said, over the rim of the cup. "Ain't seen 'im since."

Turning, she looked directly at the sheriff, who avoided her stare by studying the black coffee. "What kind of trouble, or shouldn't I inquire?"

"Trouble at Mabe's, some nonsense with a couple of new boys in town."

"B.Z., sometimes I think you ain't got the brains that the good Lord gave a chicken. What did you have that poor boy doin' up in a place—"

"He came running back that there was trouble up there, and then when I was breakin' it up, he just came runnin' in," the sheriff interrupted. "Oh, he was bound and determined to do someone damage, holdin' a walkin' stick like a sword in one a those picture books."

Shiloh couldn't help noticing that the sheriff was having a hard time keeping a smile off his face with the memory of the previous night's disturbance.

But the landlady wasn't smiling. She was staring back at the sheriff with eyes as cold and hard as quartz. It only took a second's glance at those eyes to drain the smile from the sheriff's face.

"It's a sin, a mortal sin how you are goin' 'bout raisin' that boy," she said. "Running 'bout all hours of the night. Consortin' with the likes as you find in that house, ringin' that bell. 'Spect he'll grow up just like your friend here, the hired killer."

"Ma'am, I would be obliged and grateful if you could figure some other way to call me," Shiloh said, setting his coffee down.

Her attention shifted suddenly from the sheriff to Shiloh. And once again, he was given a good long stare from those hard little eyes, but Shiloh did not look away. In them he could see a life of hard times and a lot of years alone, but there was no bitterness in those eyes. Not a trace of the kind of bitterness Shiloh had seen in the eyes of women who had lived a long time on their own.

"I'm sorry, Mr. Shiloh. Was unfair of me to judge you before givin' you your say."

"Mr. Shiloh here was in the war, with the Union, I believe. Isn't that so, Mr. Shiloh?" the sheriff interrupted, glad that the topic of conversation had drifted away from Amos.

"That's right."

"A boy I knew a long time ago was in the war," the landlady offered. "He never returned."

"I'm sorry to hear that," Shiloh said, feeling the cold familiar fear crawl up his back. With his fingers tightening around the cup, Shiloh lifted the coffee again to his mouth. Burning his lips, the hot coffee forced back the fear. When he set the cup back on the table, those two hard quartz eyes were staring at him again. They stared as if they could see right through him, to glimpse the fear and the dreams that had kept him turning in a soaking sweat through the night. But now something else was there. Around their crinkled edges Shiloh thought he could see traces of kindness.

For a moment Shiloh thought she would say something more about the war. *It must have been terribly hard*, she seemed to want to say, or *You have had a time of it*. But she didn't say anything of the sort. Rising from the table, she moved quickly toward the cupboards. "Would you like a biscuit with peach preserves, Mr. Shiloh?" she asked when she finally did speak.

"Yes, ma'am, that would suit me fine," Shiloh said. Then, turning to the sheriff, "These men, were there four of them?"

"Last night? No, there was two, but they didn't do nothin' I could lock 'em up for. Some carrying on about the King of Spain and one a Mabe's girls. Even after they ran through it real slow, I couldn't make sense of it."

"They appear to be hard cases to you, Sheriff?" Shiloh asked, nodding to the landlady who laid a jam-covered biscuit in front of him.

"They was hard, maybe the men you seen rob the Fargo coach. You point a finger an' I'll lock 'em up."

"Thought you said there was two of them?"

"There's four in town, two over in Mabe's last night, now staying in back a the saloon, and two more, bunkin' over at the livery."

Shiloh took a bite of the biscuit, letting the sweet preserves melt over his tongue before answering. "Can't say for certain," he said around a mouth full of biscuit. "I shot one in the shoulder. But they kept their faces pretty well covered. Couldn't say so that it would stand up in court."

The sheriff gave a longingful look at the biscuit that Shiloh finished off in another bite, knowing now that he would not be offered one. "We could search 'em, check their shoulders for bullets and saddlebags for the money. Fargo office said there was more'n three thousand in that box."

"If they did the stealing, then they prob'ly hid the money up in the hills, some of it least ways," Shiloh speculated. "If they leave town, I'll follow them. If they stay, they'll get into trouble."

Suddenly the landlady was between them, standing in front of the empty chair and giving the sheriff a look that would freeze water in August. "You don't mind my inquirin' between all this Fargo robbing conversation, where you might suppose Amos to be?"

"Amos, I would guess he's already back up at the office," the sheriff replied. "Prob'ly sweeping out the cells and cleaning the stove. By the way, Shiloh, they brought that Fargo wagon in just a bit ago. An' that story you told me, it checks out with what the boys said."

Shiloh considered the sheriff. "If I can inquire, it isn't real usual to see a lawman dealing faro, and that boy, Amos, well, I don't think I've ever seen anything like it."

The sheriff smiled. Obviously Shiloh had hit on one of the sheriff's favorite stories. "Well, sir, it's like this," he began. "When I rode into town, what was it, ten years ago?"

"It was nine," the landlady put in from the stove.

"Nine years ago I rode into Silver Creek on the stage. I was on my way to Brodie to make my fortune at cards. An' I was pretty good too, worked my way clear across from St. Louis, I did. Anyway, no sooner do I sit down and play than I get into a little trouble 'bout the way some jasper was dealing," the sheriff said as he took a deck of cards from his pocket and began to cut them one-handed. But a stern back-turned look from the landlady caused him to replace the cards in his pocket.

"Anyway, it ended in some gunplay," the lawman continued. "Other fella, it turned out, was working a marked deck. So I wasn't found guilty of anything, least of all killing him. But two of his friends, they jumped me afterward. Took my money. My watch, everythin'."

Then the sheriff took a long, satisfying sip from his coffee, obviously enjoying the telling of his appointment to lawman. "Anyway, 'bout that time, the job of sheriff was open and I naturally applied. Next year I was voted in and I haven't been voted out yet."

"How'd the sheriff's job come to be open?" Shiloh asked as he set his own coffee down.

"That was the fella who was cheatin'," came the reply. "But his job didn't pay nearly 'nough to suit me, so I worked out an arrangement with the Native Son. They staked me first off, now I bank the game."

"And Amos?"

The sheriff's tone changed at this part of the story. His voice grew softer and serious, both. "His folks, good people, went an' died 'bout eight years back. We just sorta took to each other."

The sheriff was right. Amos was back at the office. But he wasn't cleaning out the cells. He was working the action back and forth on one of the sheriff's breechloaders, figuring that it may come in more than a little handy for capturing the road agents.

When the sheriff came in, he saw the boy at the gun rack and walked over to him. Laying a hand gently on his shoulder, he said, "Thinkin' 'bout tradin' in your cane for a rifle?"

Amos turned to the sheriff and stared up at him. The look on the youngster's face was all the sheriff needed to know that the boy had taken it hard.

"I'm sorry, son, I 'preciate what you was tryin' to do last night. But it wasn't nothin' that I couldn't handle."

The boy continued to stare at him, moving backward and out from under the hand on his shoulder.

"What do you say we take off for a little while, next week maybe? Do some huntin' up in the mountains?"

Turning again to face the sheriff, Amos seemed visibly

brightened by this. The sheriff pressed on, "Go up to that old line shack, maybe fish too, I'll do the cookin'."

Making a comical face of disgust at the mention of the sheriff's cooking, the boy pointed to his own chest and then smiled.

"That's a deal then, you do the cooking. Now, you go on about your business. I ain't seen you doin' your reading today."

The boy gave the sheriff a mournful look and picked up the week-old newspaper. The lawman, striding around behind his desk, sat lightly in the chair and began to read the circulars and dodgers that had arrived with the weekly mail. Next week, he knew, there would be another paper for the boy.

But Amos did not read the paper. Staring at the gray print, the words swirled before his eyes. He was safe behind the thin gray wall of paper. Safe from the sheriff and those keen eyes that could always spot a lie, sometimes before it was even told. Behind the paper, which he rattled and pretended to read, he was thinking of the livery and a small opening beneath the stairs, not big enough for a grown man, but certainly big enough for him and close enough to hear every word the outlaws muttered.

17

SHILOH WAS DRINKING at the Native Son Saloon when the sheriff walked through the batwing doors. He was wearing a big smile and shuffling a deck of cards with a *mille fleur* backing easily from one hand to the other.

A half-dozen howdies greeted the lawman before he had taken three steps into the bar. Slowing as he approached the faro table, he saw no takers and continued walking to where Shiloh sat alone at a back table.

"You find that boy, Sheriff?" Shiloh asked, bringing his hat back a notch on his head before taking a drink.

The sheriff sat, shuffling the cards slowly and noting with pleasure the intricate patterns that passed from hand to hand. "Sure did, back at the jail. Humbled and red-faced as all git out. Care for a game?"

"If I did, and if I had the money, you know it wouldn't be with that deck," Shiloh replied with a small smile, now recognizing the cards as one of the Grandine company's products. He knew that it was no coincidence that the company also sold hideaways as well as their special cards and dice.

Fanning the deck out in one hand, the sheriff pretended

to study the cards closely, looking for imperfections. "Perfectly good cards, fifty-two of 'em. Mail-ordered all the way from New York."

"Mind if I take a look at them?" Shiloh asked as he extended his hand.

The sheriff drew the cards together with one hand, laid them down on the table, and pushed the neat stack across to Shiloh. "You see, son. I got myself a situation here, I was hoping you could clear up."

Shiloh began dealing the cards across the table. His hands worked quickly as he turned out the cards into four stacks. "Now what would that be, Sheriff?"

"Oh, a little matter of Wells, Fargo & Company bein' a bit particular 'bout havin' their loyal and trusted employees shot. Not to mention, the men themselves. They were mighty fine customers of mine and friends."

Shiloh continued to deal the cards, working his way steadily through the deck. "That is a problem."

The sheriff watched Shiloh work the cards, then stopped the deal to take the top card from one pile and place it on another with a satisfied nod. "Now I got myself five strangers in town, you and four others. And I got myself a pretty good notion that one or alla you five is the ones who shot the Fargo man."

"That's a fair notion," Shiloh replied, dealing out the last card. "Almost like a poker game, isn't it?"

"Almost, but I ain't playin' with my deck. An' that makes me a mite nervous."

"If this is the deck you play with, then I reckon you should be nervous," Shiloh answered as he turned over and fanned the first stack of cards across the table. They were all hearts. The ace was first up.

The sheriff nodded at the red cards. "Naw, that deck there, that's just for fun. Belonged to another sheriff, usta work here. But the Fargo people, they ain't the kind ta fun. An' in this game, I ain't neither."

Shiloh turned and fanned the second stack. They were diamonds. "I don't see the problem. You got a fist full of telegraphs saying I ain't a road agent."

"No, son, what I got is a mess a telegraphs sayin' this fella Shiloh ain't. But I ain't sure you're even him."

Shiloh turned over the clubs and fanned them out. "You know that ain't true."

"Seein' as we ain't playin' with my deck, I ain't sayin' one way or another. But if you are this Shiloh bird, then I figure you got some work in town."

The spades came up last. "If them other four are the ones that took the stage, I suppose I do. But Fargo don't pay off on *ifs*."

"They do if a sworn-in sheriff swears that they the ones that did the killin'."

Studying the cards, Shiloh smiled slightly before mixing them smoothly back together and handing them across to the sheriff. "That ain't my game. I don't work for ifs neither."

"But if you think that those are the men—"

"Sheriff, you got a whole stack a telegraphs in that office down the street. Which one of them do you think would back me up in court?"

Behind the sheriff's poker-player face, the clockwork gears of his mind turned as he thought over the question. "I reckon you know them fellas better'n me."

Shiloh poured himself another drink from the bottle. "I know 'em well enough to take their money for what I do. I know them well enough to know that in the whole bunch of them, not one would raise a little finger to keep a judge from passing sentence or me from takin' the slack out of a hangman's rope."

"But if something were to happen to those fellas?" the sheriff asked. "Something, say, in the middle a the night."

"I don't work for nothin'," Shiloh answered. "And you ain't talking my game. The dodger I saw on the two brothers didn't say '*Dead* or Alive.' "

The sheriff lifted the mail-order deck halfway up to eye level and squinted at the cards. "You jest figure on lettin' something happen then? Something profitable?"

"If that's the way you're fixing to look at it, that's about it, Sheriff," Shiloh replied, then drained his glass. "I got a score to settle with them, but I ain't the law. Now, on the other hand, you are the law. You could jail them for spitting the wrong way. Wait for the judge to pass through and maybe even get them out of town. I reckon you got a good half-dozen ranchers and like that could help you out on that."

Shiloh saw them before the sheriff. Follard and Burrows walked through the batwings into the saloon, their appearance dropping a sudden quiet over the mirrored room. Shiloh could feel his hand inching toward the gun at his waist, even as he watched the sheriff cut and recut the marked deck. He worked the cards over smoothly in one hand, his fingers moving mechanically, like a small steam engine. Shiloh couldn't see the sheriff's other hand, the one that had dropped beneath the scarred surface of the table.

As the two outlaws passed the table, the bigger one leaned slightly, lowering his shoulder toward Shiloh, before the smaller one laid a hand on the other shoulder.

"Afternoon, Sheriff," the smaller one said.

The lawman stopped working the cards and dealt one that skidded across the table toward Shiloh. "You boys enjoying the hospitality of Silver Creek?" he asked.

"Nice town, real pleasant," Follard replied, pausing a

heartbeat beside the table before moving on with his large companion.

The sheriff dealt out another card. "That's fine, boys, real fine. You jest let ole B. Z. Walker know if there's any little thing I cain help you with."

"That we will, Sheriff, that we will," Follard replied. And then they were gone, vanishing through the back door and into the small room they had rented.

Once again the wheels turned behind the sheriff's stony face, then he smiled. "Them runnin' 'round like that makes a man want to settle a score immediately. Don't it?"

Shiloh studied the two cards the sheriff had dealt him. Ace of spades and ace of diamonds. "Not if it means hangin'; those two weren't the brothers in the dodger," he said and sent the two cards skidding back across the table, smooth as a Virginia City dealer. "But doesn't it make a respectable lawman want to tidy up his town a bit? I would suspect it makes a sheriff want to open that drawer in his office and snatch up a whole fist of deputy badges. Hand them out to the first six men he met on the street."

"I ain't got 'nough good gun hands for the likes a them. Then again, I could deputize you."

"Sheriff, I think I'd rather play you for my last nickel, blindfolded and usin' those cards, than pin on a badge."

The sheriff's face did not change expression as he pulled his chair back from the table and stood. "It's been a pleasure talkin' to you, Shiloh. I reckon I'll see you in town, long as your money holds out."

"Sheriff, I reckon you will."

As the sheriff walked to the door, Shiloh could distinctly hear the soft rustle and snap of the trick cards that the sheriff shuffled nervously between his two large hands.

• • •

"Sam, it hurts like hell, Sam," said the big man, pleading, almost like a child. "An', Sam, I doan feel too good. All hot and like."

"Quit bellyachin' and let me see it," Follard replied.

"Sam, I got the chills like," Burrows replied. "He shot me bad."

By lantern light, Follard unwrapped the bandage that protected Burrows's shoulder wound. He wasn't surprised that it hurt. The day before he had cut a patch of sickly moss from the side of a tree and told the fool it was Indian medicine. The moss had stopped the bleeding and for a time Follard thought that it might just work.

But now, as he peeled off the gray poultice, Follard could see that it had not worked. It was a clean wound, in and out. Two days without proper doctoring had taken its toll. The bullet hole oozed a thick, sickening pus. Around its edges the wound's infection spread in a green-gray bruise. It stank to high heaven.

Follard had seen wounds like it before, and he knew that even with doctoring, Burrows would lose the arm. More likely he would die anyway. Sam knew that whatever he would have the big man do, it better be fast. In another day Burrows wouldn't be good for anything, that is, if he was still alive.

"It doesn't look too bad, my friend," Follard said, pulling his head away from the rotting stench of it. "And you're sweating, that's real good. Means that Indian medicine is working."

"Sam, I cain hardly lift my arm, and I doan feel proper. I feel right poorly."

"Pshaw, I've seen ladies hurt twice as bad that didn't complain half as much," Sam said, turning away from the putrefied wound. "As long as you can move it, you'll be all right. Have a nice scar to show the ladies."

Turning his head sideways, the big man took his first look at the wound. The sight made his eyes open wide with animal terror. "Sam, put that Indian moss back on, I need it. Please, Sam."

"Okay, but you haven't forgotten about our friend out there, that saddlebum jasper? Have you?"

"No, Sam, I ain't forgot. How come it smells like a daid cat, Sam?"

Lifting the chunk of blood-soaked moss, Sam placed it against the wound. Then, nearly gagging from the rotten meat smell, he forced himself to reattach it to the wound with the rag, now dyed a dark brown from the blood.

"Now then, we are going out there and have ourselves a little drink," Follard said, wiping his hands on his trousers. "And I'm paying. Then you are going to take care of some unfinished business with that fella."

18

SHILOH SAT FACING his landlady in the kitchen of the boardinghouse. The small, warm room was filled with the smell of fresh-baked bread and the rich aroma of the stew that bubbled thickly on the stove. "Seems to me you're a mite short on boarders today," Shiloh said, watching as the landlady stirred and fussed over the stew, turning up the large chunks of meat with a long-handled spoon.

"Had most move out this afternoon," she answered, not turning from her vigil at the stove. "The two that are left requested to take their meals in their rooms."

The fresh loaf of bread on the table smelled delicious. Dusted with flour, it reminded Shiloh of how his momma made it. So soft and rich you didn't need butter, preserves, or molasses. Now, half drunk at suppertime, he had to fight back the urge to rip a great, soft steaming chunk from it and stuff it into his mouth. "That wouldn't have anything to do with me, now, would it?"

"I suspect it does, Mr. Shiloh," came the answer in a weary voice. "I truly suspect it does."

"Then I am sorry, ma'am," Shiloh said, still staring at the bread. "But you tell them, I'll be moving along soon."

She did not answer him directly. Instead, turning from the stove with a large bowl of stew, she set it down in front of him. "I see that you are in the habit of not wearing your pistol to the table, Mr. Shiloh."

"Is there a reason I should?" he answered, dipping his spoon into the stew.

She was at the table again, this time setting down a jar of molasses and the salt mill. "None that I can possibly imagine," she replied, turning back to the stove.

"Me neither," came the voice at the door. It was a thick, sneering voice that caused Shiloh to nearly drop his spoon, halfway to his mouth.

Turning his head slowly, Shiloh watched as Burrows stepped through the door. He was walking half stooped, his right hand wrapped around the pistol that was wedged in the front of his pants, cross-draw style. "You are one daid sonofabitch," Burrows said, pulling the gun out. "You alraidy daid and gone to hell."

Before Burrows had the gun raised, Shiloh leapt up, turning over the chair. His hand inched toward the knife at his back.

"You jest stay there; you daid 'ready," Burrows said, pulling the trigger. The shot streamed past Shiloh's legs, hitting the iron stove and careening off into the cupboard to shatter a small stack of plates.

Shiloh could see now that Burrows was sick. Sweat poured down his face and soaked through the faded blue shirt. The blast from his gun had sent him stumbling backward a half step toward the door.

"You're sick, boy. You just take it easy," Shiloh said in a whisper. "You just put that gun down."

The landlady scampered past the two men and toward

the parlor. Somewhere at the front of the house a door slammed.

Shiloh drew the knife slowly from its sheath.

"I reckon I be sick all right, but you daid," Burrows croaked as he took an unsteady step toward Shiloh. He was blinking now against the salty sting of sweat that ran down into his eyes from under the wide-brimmed hat and matted hair. "You daid, you bastard."

Burrows's arm came up slowly, as though the pistol weighed fifty pounds. There was less than two yards between the men. So close that Shiloh could smell the rotting stench of the wound and the sickly sweat of the man. "What is it that's ailing you, boy?" Shiloh asked, the knife's blade set low and flat against his leg.

"You daid, daid, daid, daid," Burrows croaked again through pale lips.

As Burrows took another step forward, Shiloh saw his chance. Moving quickly, he brought the knife up and out from his body, even as he sidestepped away from the pistol's barrel.

But Shiloh's knife, aimed dead center at Burrows's ample gut, stopped short. Instinct, directed by the big man's clouded vision, brought his gun hand up at the last second to block the razored edge of Shiloh's knife. The blade caught the arm just below the elbow.

For an instant both men stood frozen as the gun tumbled from Burrows's twisted fingers and fell to the floor. The blade of Shiloh's knife, buried nearly to the hilt, protruded bloody through the arm that was already numbed with infection. Shiloh felt the heavy, quivering weight of the big man through the steel blade and bone handle.

Then Burrows erupted in a rage of animal fury, his mouth twisting open in an inhuman bellow of hate and pain. Raising both arms from his side, he swung wildly with his free hand. Shiloh brought the knife up, impaled through the outlaw's raised arm. Blood streamed down the worn handle of the knife and across Shiloh's face. With his other hand, Shiloh pushed against Burrows's chest, but despite the pain, the big man kept coming, edging Shiloh back in stumbling steps.

Burrows brought his other hand up; its fingers rolled tight into a great, scar-covered fist. Shiloh pushed out with all his strength against the outlaw's chest to no avail. Then, twisting the blood-soaked handle of the knife, he felt the scrape of the blade against bone. If Burrows felt the pain, he did not show it. Shiloh saw the blur of the fist as it came down, the blow striking him in the temple, sending him reeling backward onto the stove with Burrows right against him.

Through the numbing fog of the blow, Shiloh pulled the knife toward him. The effort brought the outlaw's arm straight out, the useless hand dangling limp, inches from Shiloh's face. The knife's sharpened blade tore down through the big man's arm, cutting a hunk of flesh from the arm that extended to the wrist.

A new flood of blood streamed from the wound across the stove to sizzle like spit, and down Shiloh's face, blinding him. Shiloh felt the knife come free of the outlaw's arm, tearing through the blood-drenched material of the shirt. Bringing the knife down to waist level, Shiloh raised the blade quickly from his side to stab the big man. But Burrows connected again, landing another blow to Shiloh's head. The pain jolted the knife from Shiloh's hand as the well-stoked stove behind him seered into his flesh.

Pushing out against the outlaw, Shiloh slipped from between the big man and the stove, but Burrows stumbled toward him. Again and again the blows fell against Shiloh's head as the outlaw's meaty fist sent blinding flashes of pain with each hard-knuckled blow to Shiloh's jaw, neck, and cheek. Grabbing wildly, Shiloh felt the bloody length of the outlaw's butchered arm slip through his fingers.

The two men fell through the parlor door in a tangled heap. Shiloh rose quickly as Burrows regained unstable footing, knocking over a spindle chair to get to his feet. The useless arm dangled at his side, swinging grotesquely as the outlaw stumbled toward Shiloh. "See what ya did ta me," he said thickly, laboring to raise his useless arm. "See it! Ya kilt me!"

And then he charged. He moved faster than Shiloh expected. He charged like a bull, straight on, half falling and half stumbling toward Shiloh, his good arm flailing wildly in front of him.

Shiloh tried to sidestep the charge, but Burrows caught him in the center of the parlor. The outlaw's good arm worked like a locomotive at Shiloh's back, each blow knocking the breath out of him.

But Shiloh was now giving as good as he got. Though with each blow Shiloh landed, Burrows only grunted. The two fought their way across the parlor, the outlaw leaving a thin trail of blood with each step he took toward Shiloh.

Moving backward quickly, Shiloh landed a clear blow to the big man's face, two knuckles of his fist sinking deep into Burrows's eye socket, blinding him. Stumbling back, Burrows bellowed again. Blinded in one eye, the other fevered eye stared wide open and wild as he stopped his fall against the front door frame with his good arm.

For a second he stood there, paralyzed with pain. Then he brought himself upright again. For just a moment, he looked like some bloodied and ruined visage from hell paying a social call, as he stood there in the doorway. But a second was all Shiloh needed, gathering his strength he moved in fast. Fists already out in front of him, Shiloh's boots found unsteady purchase against the parlor's clean-swept floor.

The first punch hit Burrows in the throat, sending him sprawling out across the boards in front of the house. Shiloh jumped, landing on top of him. The big man then brought his good hand up weakly, open-palmed and fingers spread; he laid it on Shiloh's chest.

Pulling back slow for a clear strike at the outlaw's head, Shiloh was caught short by a voice above him. "Now that'll be enough of that," the sheriff said. "You git yerself up offa that ole boy."

Shiloh brought his fist down and his head up just in time to see the sheriff, cutting cards one-handed with the landlady beside him, her hand brought pristinely up to her mouth in an attitude of complete horror. From farther down the street, Shiloh could hear the sound of running boots across the boards.

"You heard me, git up offa him," the sheriff repeated without missing a roll of the cards.

Burrows brought his fist down from Shiloh's chest, the arm falling heavily to the boards.

Then the sheriff stopped cutting the cards, pocketed them, and reached down. Grabbing Shiloh by the back of his torn shirt, he pulled him up off the outlaw.

"Oh, mercy, what have you done to that lad?" the sheriff asked, examining Burrows and seeing the bludgeoned face and sliced arm.

Shiloh lay next to Burrows on the boards gasping. "He 'tacked me, Sheriff, in the kitchen, ask 'er," Shiloh managed through burning lungs. "Tried ta kill me."

"Oh, heavens, my heavens," was all the landlady could manage.

Kneeling beside the barely breathing outlaw, the sheriff

tore open the big man's shirt. The moss poultice fell free, thick with yellowed pus and blood. Squinting as he examined the wound, the sheriff looked from the outlaw to Shiloh and then back again.

''Appears you done caught yerself a damn road agent, prob'ly saved the cost of a trial an' a hangin' from the looks of 'im.''

19

Amos could feel his legs begin to ache. They burned and knotted up from ankle to thigh as he crouched in the narrow hidey-hole. The small closet beneath the livery's stairs was not as large as he had first thought. Now, with his knees drawn up nearly to his chin, he wasn't sure how much longer he could stay hid. And then, too, B.Z. had been calling him. He could hear the sheriff's voice carrying in from the street, through the wide barn doors, to where he hid behind the small door.

He did not know that the sheriff had that Shiloh fella locked up in one cell, and a dead man laid out in the other, and that he needed someone to watch both while he went looking for the other three.

All Amos knew is that hours had passed slow as cold molasses since he had crept into the small space beneath the stairs. He knew from the crack under the door that it must be dark. Supper had come and gone, most likely, but he had not heard anything from the outlaws.

The smell of fresh hay was no longer sweet. The horse in the stall on the other side of the wall had been fed and well watered. A little while before, the horse had let go in a great splashing stream that leaked under the rough wood wall. Now the backside of the boy's pants was soaked through with it.

Finally, as he was deciding to abandon the closet, he heard the footsteps. They moved rapidly across the hay-strewn floor and up the creaking stairs. There were two of them, he could tell that by the sound of their boots.

The boy held his breath as the two men passed. They did not speak at first, but he was certain it was them.

"We gotta ride," one said as they moved about above the boy's head. "It was a damn mistake comin' and now we gotta leave. You saddle up on Sam's horse."

"Marcus, that sheriff, he ain't but nothin'. We cain take care a him if we do like we planned. Take the whole damned town, saloon, bank, Fargo office, just take 'em. And ta hell with Sam. And ta hell with Lester, that short, laughing sumbitch, he never show'd up anyways."

"Take the whole town?" came the angry reply. "Last week there was six a us. Six and it just mighta worked, with Sam's maps and all. Now, there ain't but three, an' I ain't sure 'bout Sam, neither. How'd three men rob a town?"

"Ya sneak up on 'er," came the reply. "Same as ya rob a man or a stage, sneak up on the sumbitch from behind through the back door."

Amos could hear the sound of bridles rustling above him. The two men were moving quickly, gathering up their outfits. "You wanna die here? That what you after, Randy? Some sheriff to shoot you or some judge ta hang you?"

"Ain't nobody gonna do no shootin' or hangin' less it's me," came the reply. "Anyways, we gotta go back ta that saloon and take Sam's money."

"The hell we do! We are ridin' outta this livery by the

back way, an' we ain't stopping 'til we see Montana. We got 'nough to get us there."

"There ain't no way you gonna see me ridin' 'way from five hundred. Not if the devil hisself was settin' on it. We walk inta that saloon and take'er. Who you suppose is gonna stop us, Sam? He tries an' the only thing he gonna stop is a bullet."

They were on the stairs now, moving slower under the weight of their saddles. "I'm ridin', brother or no, I ain't stayin' 'round to die."

The two of them passed the small closet, still bickering. Amos held his breath and closed his eyes. When he heard one of the stall doors creak open, he let his breath out slow, through his nose. And then he felt it, like a tug on his pants leg. At first it was so gentle, Amos doubted he felt it at all. When he felt it again, his entire body tensed. Then the mouse's minute claws scrambled for footing on his shin, and Amos kicked out instinctively, mouth open in silent terror as his foot slammed open the small door.

"What in hell!" cried one of the voices as two pairs of footsteps ran toward him.

They found Amos sprawled half in and half out of the small space. His eyes were wide as saucers as he looked from the mouse, which retreated under a mound of old hay, to the two pistols aimed at his head.

"How long you been listenin', boy?" the bigger one demanded, sliding his gun into its holster. "What you hear?"

Amos continued to stare, then frantically tried to scramble away, forgetting even to stand, crawling in a panic on all fours toward the door.

The one who had holstered his gun reached down and picked the boy up by the front of his shirt. "What you doin' under there, listenin' in on what folks're sayin'?"

Amos opened his mouth wide in fear. His jaw worked weakly as his mute tongue lolled half out of his mouth. From out of his mouth came a small mew, like a kitten makes, and then, in panic, a deeper grunt from down in his chest.

"What you hear, boy?" the big one said, now pinning Amos against the wall. "You better start talkin'."

"Leave 'im be, Randy," the smaller one barked, now putting his gun away. "We gotta ride."

"But he heard. He was spyin' on us," came the reply. "An' he's gonna tell the sheriff everythin'."

The big one now had Amos pinned against the wall neatly. The knuckles of the hand that held his ragged shirt dug painfully into Amos's chest. "You tell us, boy!" the outlaw threatened, bringing the boy away from the wall, then pounding him back into it. "You start talkin'!"

"Leave 'im! We gotta ride," the other put in. He was standing behind the bigger one now; reaching out, he put his hand on the big outlaw's shoulder to pull him away from the boy. But the big one just shrugged free of the grip.

Amos struggled against the large hand that pinned him against the wall, squirming uselessly this way and that. Then he kicked out, his barefoot toe striking only the top of the outlaw's boot.

Randy Stemper watched the boy struggle at the end of his extended arm. A twisted smile spread slowly across his face. The face became almost gentle for a moment as the crooked smile faded to be replaced by a small grin that showed no teeth. "Okay, let's ride. You saddle the horses, an' I'll take care a this one," he said finally.

"What you gonna do, Randy?" Marcus Stemper asked, already moving toward the horses, a saddle in each hand. "You jest tie 'im up or somethin', you hear?"

"I hear you, Brother," the big outlaw whispered as he loosened his grip on the boy's shirt.

The sheriff found Sam Follard drinking at the Native Son Saloon. He was leaning over a clean glass filled with the bar's best liquor, dressed up for all the world like a politician on election day.

"Heard you had some trouble in town, Sheriff," he said, facing the lawman and looking him straight in the eye. "Tragic affair, but all part of what makes the West wild and those dime novelist publishers in New York rich."

"Thought you might be interested to know that it involved that friend of yours," the sheriff said, moving slowly toward Follard.

"Clayton? Oh, that is dreadful," Follard said, raising his glass and downing the liquor. "And that other gent, Shiloh, is it?"

"That's right," the sheriff answered. "Your friend is dead. I got Shiloh in a cell. I don't hafta tell you how obliged I would be if you'd come back to the office to make arrangements for the dead one."

"But, Sheriff, I hardly knew the man, really," Follard said, motioning the bar-dog for another round. "Met up with him on the trail, so to speak. Just last week. Poor unfortunate, I took pity on him. He wasn't right in the head if you hadn't guessed from our little misunderstanding the other night."

"Just the same, I surely would be obliged," the sheriff persisted, his hand now resting lightly on the butt of his pistol. "Arrangements and all of that."

Follard considered the new glass of liquor in front of him. He stared down at it, nodding slowly. "If it's a matter of money, Sheriff," Follard said as he stopped nodding. "A matter of arrangements, as you say, I have several hundred dollars in my possession. Fortune has smiled down on me as of late.''

''It don't cost but twenty to get buried in this town,'' the lawman responded. ''Now I been askin' ya nice and polite, but that ain't workin' so I 'spect I'm gonna try somethin' else.''

The sheriff wrapped his fingers around the worn grip of his pistol. He moved slightly sideways, in a gunfighter stance, and pulled smoothly up on the revolver.

Seeing this, the bar's patrons made their exits, trotting quickly toward the batwings. Only the bar-dog remained, lingering safely toward the end of the bar, ready to duck at the first real sign of trouble.

''Sheriff, I assure you that will not be necessary,'' Follard said softly without turning as he lifted his drink. ''I am a gentleman, and I intend to continue to act as one.''

''Now that's nice. You just come along with me, and we'll have ourselves a little sit-down chat,'' the sheriff soothed, letting his thumb stray from the hammer of the pistol.

Follard moved slow, like a man going to jail. Downing the liquor in one gulp, he studied the empty glass and lowered it slowly to the bar. But when he brought his arm up again, he wasn't moving slow. He turned toward the sheriff quickly, a small Perry and Goddard double-header hideaway rested in his palm, his finger on the trigger and the hammer already back.

''You go directly to hell, Sheriff,'' he said as he pulled the open trigger.

The lawman had his pistol halfway up and was pulling back on the trigger when the .44 slug slammed into his leg. Staggering back, he felt the crippling pain of the bullet tear his leg out from under him. His foot splayed sideways as the bone just beneath his knee shattered. Still looking at Follard, he struggled to regain his balance, but the two pieces of the ruined bone bent neatly beneath his weight sending him to the saloon's sawdust floor.

Follard quickly swiveled the barrel and pulled back the hammer as he readied the next shot. "Gentlemen, my dear Sheriff, do not hang," Follard said in a tight-throated threat. Extending his arm up, Follard took careful aim at the lawman, squinting down the foreshortened barrel as he drew a dead aim at the sheriff's head.

But the sheriff beat him to the next shot. Raising his already cocked gun, he squeezed off a round that hit Follard clean in the stomach, pushing him back across the bar and knocking the small gun from his hand.

Follard supported himself on the bar with a palsied arm as he stared down at his brocade vest and the thick blossom of blood that spread across its front. The look on his face was one of genuine surprise and perhaps even regret of having the garment ruined.

The sheriff fired again. This time he hit Follard in the chest. Another bright circle of blood flooded out across the fabric of the vest. But Follard did not take notice of the second shot. He was dead by the time he hit the floor.

"You okay, B.Z.?" the bartender cried as he peered over the mahogany at the prone lawman. The bar-dog scurried around, his long apron fluttering as he approached the sheriff. "Who was that sumbitch, anyhow?" he asked, kneeling beside the sheriff.

"Damned if I know who any a them are, but that one weren't no goddamned gentleman."

20

FOUR MEN, DRINKERS from the Native Son, carried the sheriff out of the saloon on the faro dealer's velvet-cushioned chair, while the bartender went to tell the doctor. They carried him out through the batwings, tilted slightly back, with his gun-shot leg swinging tits-on-a-bull-useless under him.

Horses and wagons stopped for the odd group, and the small crowd that had gathered in front of the saloon parted reluctantly as they made their way over the boards and down into the street toward the doctor's office. The sheriff cursed like a drunk mule skinner as the men labored under his weight. When they were halfway across the street, they heard the yelling. It began from down the street and got louder and louder with each painful swing of the sheriff's leg.

"B.Z.! B.Z.! We got trouble," came the cry as the blacksmith pushed frantically through the small crowd of onlookers who had followed the shot lawman and his four chair bearers into the street. "Oh, Lord, B.Z., what did they do to ya?"

"Sonofabitchin', smooth-talkin' bastard shot me," the

sheriff replied as the blacksmith hustled on short stocky legs to catch up with the four men who carried the chair. As he ran up alongside, the blacksmith could see the rope that someone had tied around the sheriff's leg for the bleeding and the opened bottle that they had put in his lap for the pain. "It's bad as I ever seen, B.Z. They killed him. Killed him like ya wouldn't kill a dog or a hog!" the blacksmith moaned as he trotted alongside the sheriff's chair. "B.Z., they killed him, then they lit out. I didn't see nothin' but their hind sides as they took off south."

"Killed who?" the sheriff asked plaintively between ragged gasps of pain. "Who killed who?"

Wringing his large, callused hands, the blacksmith paused, then began running again to catch up to the chair. "The boy, B.Z., they killed Amos," he said finally. "I jest now found 'im in the stable."

"Amos?" the sheriff said uncomprehendingly. "Amos is dead?"

"B.Z., they killed him," the blacksmith tried, his voice going low in a mourner's whisper. "They gutted 'im an' left 'im in the stable."

Even the men carrying the chair paused now. Their heads turned from their task to take in the blacksmith. As tough a man as there was in town, he was standing beside them in a leather apron, wringing his hands together like an old maid. "B.Z., what kinda person does that?" the blacksmith asked, his eyes going from the sheriff to the four men and then back to the sheriff. "He weren't but a boy. What kinda person does that to a boy?"

The sheriff reached down to his lap and raised the opened bottle to his lips. Five pairs of eyes watched him as he drained off a good third of the nearly full bottle, then set it slowly back down in his lap. "I'll tell ya," he said at last. "A goddamned dead one."

Then there was silence. Every living thing in town seemed to stop. Even the men, who had labored and grunted under the weight of the sheriff and the velvet-cushioned chair, no longer seemed aware of their burden. Stopped still as stone statues in the middle of the street, they waited.

The sheriff seemed to no longer feel the pain of his near-severed leg. The blacksmith, twining his thick fingers together, still vividly saw the young boy hung up by a length of bridle to a tack post, his insides spilled out beneath him across a scattering of hay.

It was the sheriff who finally broke the silence, his eyes snapped back from someplace far away. ''Goddammit, move me, fast!'' he cursed, bringing the men back to life as well.

Once again they struggled under the burden as they made their way down the darkened street with the blacksmith following behind.

''Not there! Not there,'' the sheriff cried angrily as they continued on to the surgeon's office. ''To the jail, take me to the goddamned jail!''

The jail smelled of death. Slamming open the doors to the office, the blacksmith ran to the far wall and turned up the lamp as the four men carried the sheriff into the back room.

''Doc'll be here in a minute,'' one of the men said as they lifted the sheriff from the chair to his bed. Another lit the lamp, then turned down the flame so that the room was nearly cast back into darkness. ''You jest rest easy now. Take another drink.''

''Ya bring that fella into me,'' the sheriff barked. ''Ya bring me that Shiloh fella.''

''B.Z., you jest take yourself a drink 'til the doc comes. Maybe he cain save that leg,'' another of the men replied.

Drawing his gun from the holster, the sheriff leveled it

directly between the eyes of the man who spoke. Then very deliberately he pulled back the hammer. ''You bring me that Shiloh,'' he said in a whisper. ''Unlock that bastard an' bring 'im here.''

The man didn't need to be told twice. He and the rest of the men backed slowly away from the sheriff toward the door.

From outside the small room, the sheriff could hear the familiar sound of a cell door opening. The lawman raised the bottle for another drink; when he brought it down to rest on his stomach Shiloh was standing in the lighted doorway. The sheriff could not see his face, only the darkened form of the man with the yellow glow of kerosene lamps behind him.

''Come here, Shiloh,'' the sheriff said. ''I need to talk ta ya.''

Shiloh moved closer to the prone lawman. He moved cautiously, aware of the cocked pistol the sheriff still held, dangling off the side of the bed.

''Sheriff,'' was all Shiloh said when he was at the lawman's bedside.

''They killed the boy, Amos,'' the sheriff moaned, his voice flattened out from liquor and grief. ''Them sonsabitches killed him.''

Shiloh bent down and took the gun away from the lawman, carefully brought the hammer back down, and laid it on the table near the bed. ''I'm sorry to hear that, Sheriff,'' Shiloh said, his voice soft and filled with genuine pity, both for the boy and the sheriff.

The sheriff took another drink from the bottle. ''He was like kin, like a son ta me, can you understand that?''

''Yes, sir, I can,'' Shiloh replied. ''He was a fine boy.''

From outside the room came a sudden commotion, boots made their way across the outer office to the room, then the door burst open. ''B.Z., the doc's here,'' called a voice from the outer room.

''Send 'im in,'' the sheriff yelled back, and in a second the door opened again and a tall, gaunt man strode into the room. He was carrying a black doctor's satchel and wearing a shiny derby.

''Would you step outside, friend?'' the doctor asked as he put the satchel down on the floor next to the sheriff's bed. Then he carefully set the hat on the table, covering the pistol Shiloh had taken from the lawman.

''He stays, Doc,'' the sheriff ordered. ''We got some talkin' to do.''

''Very well then,'' the doctor replied as he turned up the lamp's wick and went to work.

''That boy was like my own, my own,'' the sheriff said, not looking down as the doctor sliced up his trouser leg with a penknife.

''Bring me some water, one of you!'' the doctor called, and immediately one of the men delivered a sloshing basin and then retreated from the room.

''I want the bastard that killed Amos,'' the sheriff whispered.

''You know who did it, killed him?'' Shiloh asked. He was crouched down now beside the bed.

''It ain't the one out there,'' the sheriff said, motioning with his head toward Clayton Burrows in the cell. ''And it ain't the one I jest shot, the dude one. It gotta be them other two.''

''This is going to hurt some, B.Z.,'' the doctor put in. ''And, you, I'll require you to hold him down.''

Shiloh stood beside the bed, then bent over the sheriff, holding him firmly down at the chest.

The doctor dipped a flour-sack towel into the basin and began to wash the sheriff's leg. He worked quickly, dipping the rag into the basin and then returning it to the bloodied leg. In a short time the basin's clear water was red.

The sheriff gritted his teeth with pain as the doctor worked the cloth around the wound. "Give him this, between his teeth," the doctor said, dropping the bloodied cloth into the basin and fetching a small, thick length of leather from his bag.

Shiloh did as he was told, forcing the leather into the sheriff's mouth. Then he put his whole weight down on the lawman as the doctor felt along the bloodied leg.

Once or twice the sheriff bucked up against Shiloh's grasp, his eyes wide with pain and face drenched in sweat. The doctor grunted as he examined the leg, his hands working over the pale length of flesh and the broken bone beneath.

Shiloh slackened his grip on the lawman when the doctor raised himself up from the bed. "I'm sorry, B.Z. There isn't anything I can do," he said, gently pulling the length of leather from the lawman's mouth.

"Yer gonna take it off, ain't ya?" the sheriff said, his voice weakened from the recent pain. "If ya gotta take it, then take it. Don't stand jawing 'bout it."

"I should do it now," the doctor offered. "Before it has a chance for infection."

"Then do 'er. I got another one anyways," the sheriff replied, his voice bitter. "Jest leave me finish my business here."

Shiloh and the lawman watched as the doctor walked to the door, opened it to reveal a crowd of faces, then shut the door behind him.

"There's a thousand dollars in gold hid out there in that office," the sheriff whispered to Shiloh. "You bring me the man who killed Amos and that thousand is yours. You unnerstand me, son?"

"I know there's two men who rode out, wanted for suspicion of murder and robbery by a sworn sheriff,'' Shiloh replied. ''If they resist I may have to kill both of 'em.''

''I already seen it, son. An' it was a fair fight,'' the sheriff said. ''You out there and outgunned two ta one. Hell, it was jest luck you happened to ride south and rest a the men rode north.''

''How do you happen to know I'll find them?'' Shiloh asked.

''Ya'll find 'em, an' ya'll kill 'em,'' the sheriff said as a new wave of pain washed over him. ''Ya'll find 'em better'n any dozen men I can round up. Now call the doctor back in here, an' tell 'im not to fergit his saw. An' you leave which ways the posse rides to me.''

The doctor, followed by three men, strode through the door as Shiloh reached for its handle. They wore grim faces, not so much as acknowledging Shiloh as they passed.

Shiloh could hear them talking behind the closed door as he took his rifle down from the rack and fished his revolver and holster from the lawman's desk. Walking out onto the boards and into the cool night air, Shiloh could hear the muffled screams of the sheriff as the doctor went to work. Without wanting to, he pictured the scene in the small room. The men would be holding the sheriff down, their faces grim and strained at the chore. The doctor, with his coat off and sleeves rolled up over his elbows, would be sawing. He would cut just above the break and if he was a skilled surgeon, it would take just over half a minute.

21

SHILOH RODE OUT of Silver Creek unnoticed and alone. The moon wasn't full, but nearly so. It bathed the gently sloping trail in darkening degrees of gray. Ahead lay the hills' night-black tree line, curving upward like a wall against a sky of distant stars. Shiloh took in the scene, thinking that it looked like the very edge of the world.

He rode the chestnut at a steady walk up the rocky trail, keeping the reins firm in his hand and prodding the beast along with both spurs. Gripping the Winchester in his right hand, Shiloh's fingers curved tight and sure around the rifle's smooth familiar stock and through the lever.

The two outlaws had left in a hurry, of that much he could be sure. Riding out of town the way they had rode into it, he was certain they would change direction at the first chance. There would be no fires to look for. They would not risk even the smallest fire to mark their camp, if they chose to stop at all. But there would be tracks. Riding fast and at night, they would not have time to obscure their trail.

And just what are you going to do if you find them?

Shiloh thought to himself. Shoot them in the back and leave the bodies out on the trail. Or shoot and fetch the pair back to Silver Creek's lawman like some damn hound? Just find them first, he decided, then see how things play. That would be job enough. Finding them would be work enough, job like hunting hair on a frog. Killing them would be the easy part, and he would have time to decide on the rest later.

For several miles out of town, Shiloh saw no tracks. Keeping his eyes shifting from left to right, and back again, he searched the rocky ground before him for signs of recent riders. Then, as he approached a small field of tall grass, nearly stirrup-high, he saw their tracks. The grass folded under its own weight and against the gentle urgings of a light breeze. Their trail was like a ditch cut through the high grass. By dawn all traces of the path would be erased by the wind. But now, in the gray light of the moon, he could see the trail through the grass as plain as could be. They had followed the trail, then left it to cut a wide swath through the grass.

But were they mule-stupid or just hurried? The two outlaws left a trail that a blind man could follow. Shiloh reined the chestnut in where the two riders had left the trail. The first tracks through the tall grass showed only one rider. As Shiloh urged the chestnut through the narrow passage across the field, he could plainly see that the trail had been started by one rider. The other had entered the field from a point farther up the trail so that their paths converged about fifty yards in from the rocky path.

As Shiloh made his way along the recent path, he noticed that where the two riders met the trail formed a rough circle of stomped-down grass. They had paused in this place, no doubt, perhaps talked or argued, their horses drawing near, then farther apart as the men carried on their business. And that done, they rode off, side by side across the field in a crooked path toward the hills.

The wide cut through the grass ended at the ragged edge of the field. At the beginning of another rock-strewn trail, they rode one behind the other again. Shiloh saw the signs of the riders as he followed the steepening trail upward. Then, later, he did not bother to look. There was no need to strain his eyes in the meager light to follow. The trail led in one direction, toward the tree line.

Turning in his saddle, Shiloh gazed back toward Silver Creek. He had ridden maybe ten miles, far enough so that the entire town, with its dim yellow points of light and dark outline of buildings, seemed insignificant against the steep slope of the night-blackened hills.

Somewhere in the vague jumble of low wooden shadows and fading lamp light was a one-legged, faro-dealing sheriff. Shiloh supposed that by now the doctor would have drugged him to a restless sleep in the back room of the jail. Perhaps one of the men stood watch over the sheriff, smoking a quirly and drinking strong coffee in the steady glow of a low-trimmed lamp.

In another room, this one darkened and silent, the remains of a mute boy would lie stretched out on a table. Come morning, if he was lucky, one of the town's women would wash him. She would work gently though quickly, thinking of the baking or sewing or chicken-feeding that needed to be done, forcing herself to put her thoughts to anything but the chore before her as she used a soft cloth, lye soap, and cold water.

Even as he imagined these things, spurring the reluctant chestnut up the rising grade of the trail, Shiloh knew that nothing would change in Silver Creek no matter what he did. He could turn off the trail and point the beast for Texas without a backward look, and nothing would change with the morning light. The lawman would lean heavily on new crutches beside the mute boy's grave. The preacher would say his words, severing the boy from the living, just as grim and businesslike as the doctor had sawed through the sheriff's leg. Then they would bury the two gunmen. And again the preacher would say his words with the same folks looking on.

And ten years hence, what would be different? The town, in Shiloh's memory, would remain as it was on the trail, not even a day's ride away and already just vague shadows in the distance.

Here it comes, Shiloh thought to himself, that old yellow coward talking at him again. He knew that cowardice first reveals itself in a teacher's voice, talking to a man as if he were a child. It curls around the brain like a fat snake and begins to whisper.

Fear, Shiloh supposed, talks loudest to men when they are alone. Generals can plot the fate of armies, safely sipping brandy as the ink dries on the paper. Ten thousand men or more will die together; their fate hidden in the educated scrawl across those sheets, many only hearing the first whispers of the demon fear as their blood stains the soil. But let a man follow what he himself knows is right, and fear will sing its sweet cowardice song in his head from the start. Fear's lies, Shiloh knew, were promises that corrupt the heart; offering men a future of riches, loving women with soft, full breasts, and a life that ends in a distant painless death.

Feeling the gentle rock and sway of the horse beneath him, Shiloh banished the coward from his head, summoning, as he had a hundred times before, the faces of the dead. The grim countenances, a memory of his dreams, were twisted into masks of unbearable pain floating like apparitions in his mind's eye. Their faces were no longer questioning, but taunting. Torn from bayonets, bullets, and grapeshot, many seemed hardly human, except for the uniforms. Blue and gray remnants, torn as indifferently as the flesh they poorly covered.

As in his dreams, many of these men Shiloh had known in life. He had heard their voices, had seen them walk and joke and move among the living. Dead, they were beyond the reach of pain, the shame of defeat, or joy of conquest. But most of all, they were deaf to the devil song of fear and cowardice.

As he thought on these things, the upward slope of the trail led Shiloh through a narrow gap toward the rocky tree line. The chestnut paused, snorting the night air from its lungs at the darkened entrance between two large stones. Shiloh spurred the beast on, stretched his fingers along the stock of the rifle, and brought his thoughts back from those of the dead.

The moon was high overhead, but offered little light on the narrowing trail. In some not very distant past, this had been the trail to Silver Creek, barely wide enough for a wagon. Shiloh guessed that it was not used much except by nearby ranchers. Presently, the rough path opened into a clearing, where Shiloh watered the chestnut and climbed down to wet his own lips at a small creek.

They had come this way, Shiloh could see that. Two pairs of horse prints were set into mud near the creek. Studying the tracks in the gray light, Shiloh could see that the two outlaws had watered their horses without climbing down.

The fresh tracks led from the creek's muddied side off through another break in the rocks and, again, up toward the tree line. Turning the reluctant chestnut from the water, Shiloh followed the tracks out of the small clearing. As he entered the narrow path, he brought the rifle up and levered in a shell. The horse's ears twitched at the double click, but it did not slow its pace.

22

SHILOH HEARD THEM before seeing them. Their angry voices carried down the rocky trail from above. And there was another sound, the harsh ring of metal striking stone followed by the grating of a shovel digging into the stone-laden earth. Shiloh had no way of knowing for sure that the men ahead were the ones he was hunting. But he would have bet on it.

Rounding a bend in the trail, Shiloh spotted the two men at a place where the tree line met the rocks. It was a long, narrow clearing that divided the rocky foothills from the forest. A natural ledge that cut neatly across the side of the hill. A scattering of trees, not quite saplings, but not grown either, ventured up the slope from the darkened forest. No bigger around than a grown man's wrist, they had found tenuous purchase in the hard, dry soil.

The voices and the sound of digging carried down the trail in the cool night air to where Shiloh pulled up the reins on the chestnut.

Though the fear was now gone, Shiloh felt his body tense with the discovery of the two men. Suddenly he could feel the small mountain breeze, scented with cedar and pine, along the opened front of his Union coat. He was keenly aware of the chestnut's twitching and anxiousness as he watched the men dig between two large stones at the base of the tree line. Their horses, still saddled, were hitched to one of the small cedars. It was not a camp, but a stop for the outlaws.

Shiloh brought the rifle up with one hand and pulled the reins tight with the other. "You boys find what you're looking for?" he asked, wedging the butt plate of the gun in the crook of his arm.

Both men turned toward the voice together. The one with the shovel dropped it clanging to the ground as the other slid his hand down to his holster.

"Don't try it. It's a fool's move," Shiloh warned as he brought back the rifle's hammer. "Just set those guns down in front of you."

"What you talkin' 'bout, mister? We know you?" the smaller one tried as his hand eased away from his holster.

"You just set them guns down, nice and easy, then we'll talk 'bout it," Shiloh suggested as he felt the chestnut strain at its bit.

"We got fifteen-hundred left in gold buried here. Ya can take half, jest for ridin' off," the other offered. "Jest pretend like, like ya didn't see us."

"I could take the whole thing, but I ain't gonna," Shiloh replied. "Now put those guns down in front of you."

Shiloh waited, letting the barrel of the rifle drift between the two men. They stood barely an arm's reach apart. If they both went for their guns at the same time, Shiloh was a dead man. He might take one of them with him, but that would be no comfort, lying on the rocky ground with a bullet in him.

"I toll you it was a fool thing, comin' back here," the

smaller one said. ''We had 'nough money. More an' enough to last.''

''Stop talking at me, Marcus. I ain't gonna hang, an' I sure as shit ain't gonna let this jasper . . .''

Before he could finish his sentence, Shiloh squeezed off a shot, the bullet chipping away at a rock three feet in front of the two men. The chestnut came up panicked on its front legs, but Shiloh pulled him in, drawing back hard on the reins as he managed to chamber another round. ''Drop them guns or you both die,'' Shiloh warned as he brought the rifle up again. ''You both die, right here and right now.''

''Hey, mister, it wasn't me,'' the smaller one said. ''It was him, he may be my brother, and it pains me to say it, but he's the one that killed that boy. I toll 'im not ta, but he did. An' he killed other ones too. Don't shoot, and I swear the sheriff'll hear the whole thin' from me.''

As he spoke, the smaller one began to reach hesitantly for his gun, drawing his hand first out from his body, then in and around toward where the pistol rested between the worn pants and his belly.

The next happened quick, so quick that later it would be a hard job to remember it all.

''You ain't no damn brother, an' you ain't no better than a dog,'' the big one bellowed and went for his gun.

Shiloh triggered off another round, but with the sudden commotion, the chestnut came up again, sidewheeling out as Shiloh pulled leather with one hand and dropped the rifle with the other. With its first steps back, the horse lost its footing on the gravel and went down, sending Shiloh sprawling painfully across the rocks.

For an instant the big one watched as Shiloh lost the horse under him, then, gun already out, he turned quickly and shot his brother. ''You ain't but a dog!'' Randy Stemper screamed as he pulled the trigger, sending Marcus staggering back toward the rocks with a bullet in his gut. "A damn dog!"

Twice more the big man fired at his brother. The first shot hit him high in the arm, the second glanced off a rock near his head. The smaller one, Marcus, watched in horror as his brother strode toward him, Shiloh now forgotten as a rage took hold.

"Ya a dog! I gonna shoot ya like a dog," Randy bellowed, advancing on his cowering brother.

Shiloh struggled away from the fallen horse that moaned and wimpered, its legs pounding furiously as it tried to regain its footing.

"You hold it there," Shiloh said, pulling the gun from its holster, and stepped over to the rifle. Lifting it, Shiloh could see that the walnut forestock was neatly split from the fall. The hammer, too, was damaged, its end chipped. As he hefted the familiar weight of the rifle, Shiloh ran his thumb quickly over the hammer and felt it jiggle under the slight pressure.

Discarding the rifle, he approached the two men, pistol drawn. The one who had been shot was bleeding bad. His face shone ghostly pale in the dim light. His hands up, palms forward, as if he could stop bullets with them. Now, both brothers looked at Shiloh, one with crazed eyes, the other with a face that was pleading, begging for his life.

"You drop that piece. I won't ask again," Shiloh said, walking closer, the gravel crunching beneath his boots.

"He's crazy, mister," the pleading brother moaned. "He ain't right, shoot him! Shoot him 'fore he kills us both!"

"Shut that damn mouth," Randy Stemper hissed, then turned to Shiloh with a crooked smile. "Come on, ya sumbitch, let's get at it."

Looking the outlaw in the eye, he made his choice. Shiloh dropped to his side and rolled as the trigger beneath his thumb went slack. When the hammer fell on the cartridge he was halfway to the ground, the outlaw's bullet whizzing close by his ear and ricocheting off the rocks behind him.

Firing again at the outlaw, now obscured by gun smoke, Shiloh heard the second shot skim off the rocks.

Then, through the clearing smoke, Shiloh could see the outlaw. He was still standing, gun outstretched in front of him, wavering as he struggled to put Shiloh in his sights. A thin line of blood ran down one side of his face, from forehead to jaw. "Sneakin', sumbitchin' bastard," Randy Stemper whispered, drawing back on the hammer with his thumb.

Shiloh fired again and missed as the outlaw suddenly dropped. The gun leapt from Randy Stemper's hand with the discharge as his legs went out from under him. His brother had hit him square in the neck with a stone.

"Kill him now, he's crazy!" the injured brother yelled.

Shiloh was on the outlaw in four strides. He kicked the gun away from the hurt man's reach, sending it scuttling over the gravel as he held his own, outstretched and pointed at the downed man.

"Looks like you win it," Randy Stemper moaned as his eyes came open to see Shiloh standing over him. "Jest shoot me and git it over with."

"Get yourself up," Shiloh said, stepping back as the outlaw raised himself on elbows.

"What's wrong with ya?" the wounded brother yelled from the rocks. "Kill 'im! Kill 'im!"

Shiloh's eyes drifted from the downed man for just a second. But that was long enough. Randy Stemper brought his boot up suddenly, catching Shiloh's wrist and knocking the gun upward. Before Shiloh could bring the Colt back down, the outlaw hit him across the ankle with his other boot, knocking Shiloh's leg out from under him and bringing him to the ground.

In a flash the outlaw was on him, scrambling up his chest, one hand wrapped around Shiloh's throat, the other trying to pry the gun from his fingers. Stemper had barroom brawler hands, the fingernails on his thumb and little finger grown out and sharpened to points. They cut like small knives at Shiloh's neck, digging into the flesh, opening two deep bloody gashes. Bringing his knee and free hand up, Shiloh managed to push the outlaw away, loosening the savage grip around his throat. Then feeling the gun slipping from his fingers, he triggered off the last three shots.

Now, with his gun hand free, Shiloh caught hold of the outlaw's own throat, just under the chin, and pushed his head back, squeezing for all he was worth. Stemper brought the gun up and leveled it at Shiloh, clicking off three rounds before he realized it was empty. As Stemper raised the gun, bringing it back over his head to use as a club, Shiloh pushed off with his knee. The outlaw fell back heavily, Shiloh helping his backward movement with a boot to the stomach.

Stemper landed on his back, but quickly turned to face Shiloh in a crouching position nearly identical to the one Shiloh had assumed. Both men were gasping for breath, looking at each other from a distance of four or five feet.

Shiloh could see now that his bullet had made a narrow crease in Stemper's forehead. His face was a bloody mask, through which two insane eyes glowered in the gray light.

Reaching behind him, Shiloh went for his knife, just as Stemper pulled the knife from his boot. Both men rose slowly to their feet, knives low and out from their bodies, the blades held flat with the cutting edge pointing inward.

Then they began to circle. Legs parted with their feet planted firmly, they shuffled in an awkward circle over the rocky ground.

"Gonna cut you bad, you bastard," Stemper wheezed as he motioned in a slow circle with his knife. The blade caught and flashed in the dim light with each small movement of the outlaw's wrist. "Gonna make what I done to that boy look like nothin'. Like a present you give a girl."

Shiloh didn't answer; instead, testing the outlaw's nerves, he inched closer. Stemper tensed, but didn't move back.

"Come on, you bastard, come on," Stemper whispered. He was smiling now. Gray teeth revealed themselves as the bloodied lips parted.

Now, with his free hand extended, Shiloh motioned quickly in a slashing move, but the outlaw's eyes didn't leave the blade in his other hand.

"You know, it's gonna be a fine day when they hang you," Shiloh said, cutting the outlaw's tentative advance off with a rapid cross slash of his blade. "Gonna be a nice spring day. Folks'll bring baskets with fried chicken, roast beef. All the ladies lookin' their finest."

"They ain't gonna hang me, you sumbitch," Stemper spat and cut his knife viciously back and forth.

"You ever go to a proper hangin'? Not some sheriff and three deputies under the cottonwood event, but a real hangin'? Nothin' is finer."

"You bastard," Stemper whispered and came in fast. Shiloh moved quickly to the side, catching the outlaw on the wrist with a fast downward slice and opening a small wound, then moving away.

"In a town like Silver Creek, a good hanging builds a

real civic spirit,'' Shiloh said with a slow smile. ''That's a real pleasure to see in a town.''

''Bastard,'' Stemper moaned and tried again, this time higher, at throat level. Shiloh caught him halfway up his knife hand, opening a tear in the outlaw's dirty shirt, but not hitting flesh.

''Even the ladies like it,'' Shiloh confided. ''Oh, they say they don't, but they watch. Have a fella up there swinging all purple-faced and twitchin' and they watch, the ladies do.''

''I'm gonna kill ya,'' Stemper bellowed and moved in again. He came in low, slicing up the air in front of him.

Shiloh backed carefully away, then turned, keeping in the circle. He moved slowly, the blade still out from his body and low, with one hand raised for the chance to catch the outlaw's knife hand.

When the outlaw realized it was useless, he stopped slicing in front of him and backed off.

''You know,'' Shiloh began again. ''About those ladies, maybe you can help me figure this. You have a fella up on the rope, maybe his neck is broke and maybe it ain't. He's all purple and his eyes bulging out. And he's kickin' like they do. And the ladies, they watch, but then they all turn away. Every time. Know when they turn away, friend?''

''When, ya sumbitch?'' Stemper answered as he moved in close, the blade once again making slow circles.

''Now I noticed this myself,'' Shiloh confided, bringing his voice low and confidential as he raised the knife, looking for an opening. ''They all look away when the fella messes himself. Ain't that somethin'?''

Stemper seemed to consider this new information for a second, his shuffling feet nearly comin' to a halt.

Shiloh saw his chance then, moving in fast and to the

left as the blade in his right hand cut across quickly at neck level.

At the sudden advance, Stemper stumbled back, bringing his knife up to block the lunge. Shiloh's blade caught him solid on the hand, cutting to the bone across the outlaw's little finger.

For an instant the outlaw released his grip on the knife, its already bloodied handle sliding from his hand. But before it could completely escape his grasp, the other hand came up and caught it in a well-practiced border-shift.

"Bastard," Stemper moaned, looking at his slashed hand and its two fingers that dangled nearly useless. "Bastard!"

"So, is that it?" Shiloh asked, moving in again. "You want me to whittle on ya all night. That your idea of a good time?"

But Stemper didn't answer. With his right hand in front of him he moved in quick, crossing the short distance that separated the two men. Shiloh backed off a step, then brought the knife forward in a sudden jab. The blade caught Stemper's right hand, now raised for a blow, slicing an inch or more down between his middle fingers before sliding off as the outlaw extended his arm.

"Bastard, sumbitch," Stemper moaned, feeling the pain of the new wound jolt up his arm. With his good hand, Stemper lunged awkwardly forward as Shiloh sidestepped the blade that flashed close to his side. Stemper followed Shiloh's sideways movement like the experienced brawler he was. Stemper's bloodied hand was extended out in front of him, its sharpened thumbnail looking for an opening as well.

With the knife in his left hand, Stemper slashed awkwardly at Shiloh who backed away easily in a flat-footed knife-fighter's jig. Stemper kept coming, using his left hand with the knife and his right with that thumb. Shiloh slashed across at the outlaw's right hand, as he danced heel-toe backward. Twice he caught Stemper near the wrist, but doing no real damage as he sliced the flesh and bloodied the frayed cuff of the outlaw's shirt.

Then Shiloh stumbled, his boot heel catching on a rock. Stemper saw the opening and took it, advancing fast with his left hand that held the knife. At the last moment, Shiloh raised his own left arm, and felt the point of the outlaw's blade bite through the rough material of the Union jacket and into his flesh just above the wrist.

Regaining his footing, Shiloh brought his blade up, grazing the knuckles of the outlaw's left hand. It wasn't a deep cut, but enough to open the fingers and send the weapon to the ground.

Shiloh lunged again, but before his blade could connect, the world went black as Stemper struck him across the side of the head, sending Shiloh's knife tumbling from between his fingers.

''Sumbitch!'' Stemper yelled as he threw himself on Shiloh. The outlaw's weight hit him like a locomotive.

When Shiloh opened his eyes, the outlaw's blood-covered face was inches from his own. The force of Stemper's charge had pushed Shiloh back. Over the outlaw's shoulder, Shiloh could see both knives, lying in the gravel behind him.

They were too close now for fists. Shiloh grabbed Stemper by the wrist and tried to turn him, but he slipped free. Pushing hard, his boots struggling for a hold on the gravel, Shiloh moved the outlaw backward. As Stemper struggled, he turned his head slightly, giving Shiloh a clear view of the crease the bullet had made in his head. Another inch and Stemper would have been dead, Shiloh thought to himself bitterly.

Then the outlaw opened his mouth wide, but no words emerged. Craning his head like a snapping turtle, he moved his mouth forward to bite at Shiloh's face. His foul breath came out in gasps.

Shiloh tucked his chin down on his chest. Then brought it up fast catching Stemper on the jaw with enough force to send him staggering backward.

Now it was Shiloh's turn to advance. He came in quick, with both fists pumping. The first blow caught the outlaw just below the eye. The second landed square on Stemper's mouth. Shiloh could feel the jagged bite of teeth collapsing, tearing upward from their roots under the force of the blow.

Again the outlaw staggered back, and again Shiloh hit him, bringing his fist around fast to catch him directly on the head wound.

Stemper bellowed, his swollen lips opening to emit a thick spray of blood that had collected in his mouth. Then he began to gag. Straining for air, the big man bent nearly double with the effort, backing away from Shiloh in a stumbling retreat. When he opened his mouth again, a fresh flow of blood poured forth with two long gray teeth at its center.

Stemper stood paralyzed as Shiloh moved in on him, fists up and head down. Then the outlaw spotted the Winchester lying on the ground. In a panicked jump he dove for the weapon, snatching it up in his bloodied hands and turning it on Shiloh. "You all but had me, Lord but I thought you did," he wheezed as he pulled the trigger.

Shiloh stopped in his tracks as the broken hammer clicked down useless on a cartridge. Stemper jacked another shell into the chamber and tried again. And again came only the disappointing click.

Shiloh began to advance once more as the outlaw clicked

off three more rounds. Realizing the rifle was useless, he turned it butt first toward Shiloh and began swinging.

The new weapon gave the outlaw another burst of strength. He came forward in wide, striding steps, swinging the blood-slick barrel in front of him. ''Come on, ya, I'll scatter yer damned brains across this damn mountain an' piss on 'em,'' he croaked through his ruined mouth.

Shiloh backed off, hands open and out. Searching the ground for weapons, he saw the dull glint of the knives and pistols, now behind Stemper.

''Come on, ya bastard,'' the big man moaned as he drew nearer. When he was close enough, Stemper attacked with the force of the pain Shiloh served up to him in a stumbling charge, his hands wrapped tight around the rifle's barrel.

Twice Stemper swung the Winchester, its stock blurring in front of Shiloh as he dodged away. With each swing Stemper took another step closer.

After the third swing of the Winchester, Shiloh made his move. Half running, half leaping, he hit Stemper low, burying his shoulder into the outlaw's gut and forcing him off his feet. As they hit the ground, Shiloh reached up for the rifle, but found nothing in his frantic grasp. It had already flown from Stemper's hands.

They were both on the ground now, Shiloh's hands around the bloody throat of the outlaw. As he squeezed, Shiloh thought that the man might be dead, that the whole thing was ended. But Stemper proved him wrong. The outlaw's limp body suddenly tensed as he struck Shiloh a blinding blow to the temple with a fist-sized rock.

Shiloh opened his eyes just in time to see through blurred vision Stemper coming first to his knees, then to his feet. Scrambling away in a half crouch, Shiloh rose to his feet and once again faced Stemper.

His arm ached with the effort of raising his fists and each throbbing heartbeat felt like a drum inside Shiloh's skull. We'll both be dead, Shiloh thought to himself, we'll just beat each other to death, right here.

Gathering what little strength he had left, Shiloh advanced on the outlaw. When he was close enough, Shiloh came in low, hitting Stemper in the jaw and feeling bone crack under the blow.

Stemper staggered, the fist with the rock falling to his side, then coming back up again, slow and trembling. Stemper seemed to sway in the cool night breeze, then took a step forward as his dimming eyes followed Shiloh's half-crouched, exhausted stance. The outlaw's broken jaw hung open, a thick stream of bloody spittle mixed with the blood from the head wound and ran down the front of his shirt.

"Give it up, boy, this ain't no good," Shiloh warned him as he moved in again.

Stemper only grunted and swung wildly, his fist missing Shiloh by more than a foot.

Shiloh worked his way in close and hit Stemper again in the jaw, sending the already busted bone thrusting out at a strange angle. The second blow hit him in the throat, bringing the outlaw to his knees.

Shiloh could see that under the bloody mask of Stemper's face, his flesh had turned a deep purple. Shiloh paused, taking in burning breaths of air as the outlaw regained his feet, gasping through his ruined windpipe.

There was only one way it could go now and both men knew it. Shiloh moved in on him, fists up as he looked for an opening between Stemper's wildly swinging arms. The outlaw swayed unsteadily as he squinted through the blood and pain at Shiloh.

Out of the corner of his eye, Shiloh once again saw the two knives lying behind Stemper, and behind them and off a little to the right was Stemper's loaded pistol. Stemper swung his head slightly, saw them too, then turned back to Shiloh.

When the outlaw ran forward again, his fists were working slow and Shiloh connected three times, though one would have been enough. The outlaw swayed slightly, then fell into Shiloh, nearly sending him to the ground.

Shiloh supported him for a second, then the weight became too much and he let Stemper go. The big man slid to his knees groaning, his ruined head leaving a bloody trail down Shiloh's now-filthy shirt. Gripping the outlaw around the head, Shiloh felt the broken jaw grind and crack between his hands.

Stemper groaned again as Shiloh held the bloodied head in his hands and twisted, breaking the outlaw's neck. Shiloh backed away, arms at his side as he watched Stemper go down, facefirst in the rocky dirt.

Taking a half-dozen steps back from the outlaw, Shiloh sat. Lungs burning and a dull ache working its way up from his knuckles to elbow, he watched the dead outlaw. Then very slowly he rose, walked past the dead man to where the other lay sprawled out across a smooth rock on his back.

"What's yer name, son?" Shiloh asked, kneeling beside the dying man's head.

Marcus Stemper moved his lips into something like a smile, but not quite. A thin trickle of bloody foam ran down his cheek from his opened mouth. "Name's Stemper," he said, his breath coming in a wet rattle. "That's my brother Randy ya killed."

Shiloh didn't reply.

''Shee-it, that's okay,'' the dying man said. ''He shot me, didn't he?''

''Yes, he did,'' Shiloh said. ''You think you can make it?'' But Shiloh knew he wouldn't.

''Be a neat trick if'n I did,'' the man said and nearly laughed.

''You got any kin, people you want told?''

''Aw, I reckon not,'' Marcus said. ''Reckon I jest wanta die here, lookin' at them stars an' such.''

''I'll go fetch you some water,'' Shiloh said and rose.

''Doan bother yerself, mister, I be gone by the time ya get back. Listen, let me ask ya somethin'. Ya think there's like a heaven and hell and like that?''

The outlaw closed his eyes then. He lay so still that Shiloh thought that he was dead. Then he spoke again. ''Do ya?''

''I guess if we're lucky there is,'' Shiloh answered the dying man as honest as he could.

''Shee-it, luck's jest been nothin' but a damn rumor for me,'' the man said, then closed his eyes for the last time.

It was nearly dawn when Shiloh finished tying the two men across their horses and dug out the Fargo gold from the rocks. Climbing back on the chestnut, he pointed the beast for Silver Creek and kneed the animal forward. If he rode steady and remembered the trail right, he would reach town by noon.